PERILOUS HOMECOMING

SARAH VARLAND

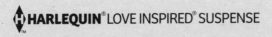

HARLEQUIN® LOVE INSPIRED® SUSPENSE

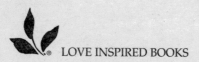

LOVE INSPIRED BOOKS

PLEASE RECYCLE · THIS PRODUCT IS RECYCLABLE ·

Recycling programs for this product may not exist in your area.

ISBN-13: 978-0-373-45690-1

Perilous Homecoming

www.Harlequin.com

Printed in U.S.A.

Every good gift and every perfect gift is from above, coming down from the Father of lights with whom there is no variation or shadow due to change.
–James 1:17

To the family and friends who have been so consistent
encouraging me as I worked to meet deadlines for this
and other books during my first year of homeschooling—
something that made for some crazy weeks.
You cheered me on, told me to eat chocolate, watched
my kids and reminded me of how much I love writing—
which I do. I'm so grateful for all of it. Thank you.

ONE

Kelsey Jackson felt the way she always did at the first rumbles of thunder on a too-hot day during tornado season. The electricity in the air was almost palpable, but not in a good way. Everything about being here tonight in this stifling room gave her one of the deepest senses of foreboding she'd ever felt. But tonight was too important for her career to let all that stop her, and Kelsey was Southern, born and bred—she could put on a fake smile, laugh lightly and be pleasant, even to her worst enemy, when the occasion called for it.

That was exactly what she was going to do tonight. No, these people weren't exactly her enemies, but they certainly weren't friends, not after they had all turned their backs on her when she left the police force and the town under a cloud of undeserved suspicion.

Just three or four more hours' worth of this prelaunch party for the Treasure Point History Museum, and she'd be almost home free. The rest of the work she'd been hired to undertake could be done in relative solitude, then she'd be back to Savannah, back to the life she'd been carefully creating there for the last six years.

"You look lovely tonight, Miss Jackson," Jim Howard, the head of the historical society, said to her as he walked past. He had a woman on his arm whom Kelsey didn't recognize.

"Thank you." She smiled as she moved away, toward the edge of the room. She'd ended up in the middle as she was walking, but being the center of attention wasn't exactly her thing. She was eager to get to the edge. That should help her feel less anxious.

But, Kelsey discovered quickly, even being at the edge of the crowded room where people in black-tie attire were mingling and celebrating wasn't relaxing. Maybe she should step outside. Get some air.

Gemma O'Dell, a former classmate who was now the museum's marketing manager, had shown her a private porch off one of the rooms on their tour of the museum earlier that day. Kelsey was fairly certain she remembered how to get to it, and from there she could step out into the cool darkness of the summer night and see if she could relax enough to get her shoulders to loosen up.

The din of voices and laughter grew quieter as she moved out of the main gallery, though there were still small clusters of people here and there in the hallways and side rooms of the museum. The way the place was set up lent itself to small conversation groups like this— it had been built to look like the antebellum plantation home that had stood on this very site for well over one hundred years, until it had been destroyed in an explosion several years before.

Kelsey moved past the library, toward the room with the porch. As she approached, she heard voices. Low. Angry?

It didn't look like she'd be alone. She should turn around, make herself go out and be social, show the town she'd made something of herself, that she had nothing to be ashamed of.

She took a deep breath, started to swivel on her new heels and walk back the way she'd come, but…

Once a law enforcement officer, always a law enforcement officer.

Four years at the Treasure Point Police Department had honed the observational skills, the attention to detail, that she'd already possessed. Voices like these deserved to be checked out.

So she didn't turn around. Instead, she walked slowly into the room, like she was just another party guest—which was true.

Her heels clicked loudly on the floor, which would have been a liability if she *was* still a police officer. The door to the porch stood open, and she could make out shapes, just barely, in the shadows. Kelsey swallowed hard as the muscles in her neck tightened and she began to feel her pulse pounding. What exactly had she planned to do without a badge and a gun?

She glanced down at herself, but sure enough, she had nothing on her that even came close to passing as a weapon. Her cerulean-blue halter dress with the swishy skirt was definitely not dangerous, and neither was the silver bracelet she always wore on her left wrist.

Kelsey hesitated a moment too long.

She heard a crash, followed by a thump, and squinted to try to make out what was happening in the dark. The shadows weren't there anymore…wait, one was. One person was climbing over the porch railing.

Where was the second?

She thought of the thump she'd heard, a sick feeling swirling in her stomach. Had that been the other person landing on the ground? The red clay on the ground was anything but soft, and even though this was only the second story of the museum, the ceilings were tall and it would be a good fall from this height.

No more investigating for her—she needed to go get help and discover what was happening outside the museum.

Her heels clicked down the hallway, and Kelsey glanced back once to make sure no one was following her. The hallway seemed clear, but she still shivered.

The noise of the party grew louder and Kelsey searched the crowd of guests to see if any of them were officers she knew from her time on the police force. There. Clay Hitchcock—one of the guys on the force who had continued to show confidence in her as an officer even when her last case had gone so wrong. She trusted him, and not just because they were cousins. Kelsey didn't mind talking to him—though there were several other men within the department she was hoping to avoid during her time in Treasure Point.

"Clay, I need to talk to you."

"All right." He nodded without questioning her, something she appreciated.

"Something's going on outside on the north side of the museum. I went looking for some air, heard low arguing, and then it seemed like there was a struggle outside on the porch."

"You didn't go out there, did you?"

She shook her head. "It didn't seem wise."

"Wouldn't have been," he agreed. "You stay here. Stay involved with the party, don't draw any attention to yourself."

Easier said than done. But Kelsey nodded, then watched for a second as Clay hurried away. She felt a longing to be back out there with a team of law enforcement brothers and sisters, helping justice win in the world. But she was used to pushing that feeling away.

She wasn't a cop anymore; she was an antiques insurance agent, one who was supposed to be wowing the historical society with her personality and giving them a quote on what her company would be able to do for them in terms of insuring the antiques and historical artifacts at the museum. Since it was a private museum and not state funded, the historical society had their pick of companies and there were more than a few in Savannah they could have called. Kelsey's boss had said that the museum's representative had specifically mentioned her by name, and so it seemed like her connection to the town—however tenuous it was right now—was possibly the reason they were being given the first chance at this job.

She couldn't mess this up. Kelsey took a deep breath, put her shoulders back and tried to remember that people didn't just care about the job you did—they cared about your personality, too. She tried to soften the corners of her mouth a bit and look less like she was scowling.

Kelsey would have been successful, too, except that when she turned to walk to the refreshments table, she ran square into one of the people from her past she would have been quite happy to forget.

"Oh, I'm sorry." The man's accent was pleasant enough. So was his voice. It was clear he hadn't recognized her yet—understandable, since her red hair was a bit tamer now than in their high school days, smoothed down and cut in an actual style rather than frizzed and messy. She'd also switched from glasses to contacts since she'd seen him last. She might feel like the same girl inside when she looked at him, but Kelsey knew she looked nothing like she had at age eighteen, which was the last time she'd laid eyes on Sawyer Hamilton.

Hamilton, as in *those* Hamiltons who owned half of Treasure Point, including the land surrounding this museum. His aunt Mary had given a small parcel of land along with the museum building to the Treasure Point Historical Society, but the Hamiltons still claimed the rest of what had been an immense estate. Sawyer, like all the Hamiltons, had always had everything.

"It's all right," she answered even though, really, was it?

In one way, yes it was. It was all right that his gaze had swept over her, taken in her face and clearly liked what he'd seen. Maybe it was petty, but Kelsey liked the affirmation of her attractiveness from the boy who had always made her feel like less, whether he meant to or not.

"I don't believe we've met." He flashed his signature grin, the one that had netted him the title of Mr. Popular in their senior class yearbook. He'd never used that grin on her before, and she was slightly ashamed at the way it gave her chills down to her painted toenails. "I'm Sawyer Hamilton."

Kelsey smiled back sweetly. Sweet like a glass of sweet tea with twice the usual amount of sugar. Stickily sweet. "We *have* met, actually. I'm Kelsey Jackson. Good to see you again, Sawyer."

At the mention of her name, his smile fell and his face paled. Still, he was handsome, with that brown hair not daring to be a bit out of place, those green-blue eyes that sparkled like he was sharing some kind of private joke with you.

Only there were no jokes between the two of them at all.

If anything, the joke had always been, and always would be, on Kelsey.

She'd grown up well—it was an understatement, but it was all his mind would articulate in that moment. "It's good to see you again, too, Kelsey."

Her eyebrows raised slightly and she shook her head. Then turned to walk away.

And then the lights went out. The hum of the electricity in the building—lights, air circulation—was gone all at once, but the gasps from people who'd been plunged into darkness without an explanation filled the void where silence would have been.

Sawyer didn't move. It was just darkness, no need to panic simply because it was unexpected—although some people were concerned, judging by the sound of shuffling feet.

He tensed as something or someone brushed his left hand. He tried to move it away, but the glancing contact turned into a firm grip from a soft, small, feminine hand.

"Sawyer?"

It was Kelsey's whispered voice. It was his turn to raise his eyebrows. A moment ago, she'd seemed eager to get away from him and now she was holding his hand? Surely she wasn't that scared of the dark.

"Yeah." He matched her low volume. "It's me."

"I need to get outside. You always carried a flashlight and a pocketknife in high school. Any chance you've got that flashlight now?"

"I've got one."

"Great. Take me to the front door?"

It was less a request than a command, but considering the fact that nothing about this situation made sense, Sawyer wasn't questioning anything at this point.

He pulled the small flashlight out of the inside pocket of his suit—glad he hadn't been able to drop the habit and leave it at home. He'd dated a few girls over the years who had made fun of his tendency to be prepared, but Sawyer liked to think it came in handy now and then.

He shone the light on the floor in front of them. Kelsey didn't release his hand, but allowed him to lead her across the mostly empty middle of the room. It seemed most of the people had pushed themselves back against the walls. There were a few other glowing spots of light in the room—apparently, despite the request from the museum board for people to leave cell phones at a table in the entryway, some people were still carrying theirs.

Finally, they reached the door.

"Thank you."

She released his hand and then she was gone, running across the lawn with her red hair, curled at the ends, flying behind her, holding her dark blue dress up above her ankles with one hand so she could run.

Kelsey hadn't run far from the blanketing darkness of the house when she ran almost straight into Clay. "Did you find anything?" she asked.

He nodded slowly, his face in the moonlight showing no signs of his usual lightheartedness or humor. "We did. Kelsey, it's Michael Wingate. He's dead."

"The curator?" Her eyes widened as she tried to make sense of what she was hearing now, what she'd seen earlier and how they were connected.

"Blunt force trauma to the head is what we're guessing right now. We won't know for sure until the ME gets him to the lab."

"Right, of course." She nodded.

"Kels? You're going to have to come to the station. Because if you were in that room and saw some kind of altercation on the balcony, you were the last one to see—or rather, hear—Michael alive before whoever killed him."

"I'm coming in as a witness, right? Not a suspect."

The look on Clay's face said all she needed to know. Treasure Point may be the place that raised her, the happy home for her growing-up years. But almost from the day she'd turned eighteen the town had been nothing but kryptonite for her, some ridiculous weakness that rendered her powerless and made her feel sick. She wished she could just turn around and leave right now. But that wasn't an option.

She needed this assignment in order to secure her place at the Harlowe Company, a prestigious antiques insurance company in Savannah. But Kelsey also needed this job to finish as quickly as possible, needed to get her feet as far away from this particular bit of red Georgia clay as she could. Treasure Point was nothing but trouble for her.

"Did you hear me?"

No, she hadn't heard anything Clay had said after she'd seen the facial expression that answered all her questions. "I didn't. What did you say?"

"If it was up to me, you'd only be a witness. But I'm afraid Davies is wanting to treat you as a suspect."

Suspect. The word she'd only narrowly managed to avoid in the case that caused her departure from Treasure Point not too many years ago. She *hated* when her integrity was questioned.

"Let's go, then." She glanced toward the museum. "Although with that lights-off stunt not too long after what I saw on the balcony, there's a good chance I'm going to need to be back here soon."

"What do you mean?"

"Something is likely missing or vandalized. It's going to be my job to assess that." Her words came out tight, pointed. She felt bad that she was directing them at Clay, one of the nicest guys she'd ever known. But the prospect of being questioned about a crime she didn't commit was enough to put anyone in a lousy mood.

Anyway, Clay was probably thinking along the same lines already. Cutting the lights was a common gambit for upscale thieves, allowing them to snatch something that had, only moments before, been in plain sight. Perhaps the curator had caught a thief in the act of tampering with the wiring prior to the blackout. Was that why he had died?

She reminded herself not to jump to conclusions. She'd barely met the curator and had been away from town too long to know the current gossip. There could be a dozen reasons someone might have wanted the man dead.

Before she could apologize, before Clay could reply, another man walked their direction, tall and a little intimidating. Lieutenant Davies.

"He read you your rights yet?"

Kelsey couldn't stifle her laugh. "Rights? Davies, I used to work with y'all. I know my rights and if you have a brain in your head, you'll realize I'm innocent."

"Are you verbally assaulting an officer?" His serious face didn't change. He'd always been a man who'd done his job well, but personally he and Kelsey had never gotten along.

She shook her head. "You know I'm not. But you also know I'm not a killer."

"I guess we'll see. I'll spare you the cuffs, anyway, as long as you move slow. Let's go get in the car."

Kelsey followed him without another word. She climbed into the *back* of the police car—definitely a first for her—and looked out the window, at the museum, for as long as she could before they drove out of view.

Straight to the place where she'd first started to realize she might not be good at everything she put her hand to. She'd already faced disgrace at the Treasure Point police station. Was she about to face murder charges there, too?

TWO

Sawyer had gone back inside after watching Kelsey exit. But though the lights had come back on in short order, the party atmosphere had already vanished. All the guests had been herded into the main gallery, where the police had announced that no one would be allowed to leave until everyone had given a statement.

That had been over an hour ago. A young police officer Sawyer didn't recognize had taken down his contact information and asked him some questions about the party—what his connection was to the museum, what he had seen and heard, who he had talked to. The kid had been annoyingly vague when Sawyer had tried to ask some questions of his own—namely, asking what on earth was going on. Clearly something wasn't right here. But none of the guests he'd spoken to in the past hour had the slightest idea what the problem was, and the police were being very closed-mouthed.

He wanted answers, and while he seldom used his family name to his advantage, he started looking around for a Treasure Point police officer who might give him some information.

There. Clay Hitchcock. No use of his family name would be necessary, since the two of them had been friends, had played football together back in high school—Sawyer was the quarterback to Clay's receiver.

"Clay!" Sawyer jogged in his direction. "I need to talk to you."

"Is it about all this?" He gestured around him. "Because otherwise it needs to wait."

"I'm not sure. Kelsey…"

"What about her? Did she tell you something?"

"No, she didn't. I just… She seemed really shaken up when the lights went off. She went from acting like she hated me to asking for my help and I don't understand what happened or where she went. I haven't seen her since then, which is weird, since I know y'all aren't allowing anyone to leave."

"You spoke to her after the lights went out? What did she want?"

"Just for me to use my flashlight to help her find her way to the door."

"So you helped her and then?"

"She ran."

Clay nodded. "I saw her after that. She's at the station now."

"The *police* station?" Sawyer frowned. "Is she okay?" Nothing about this was making sense to him.

"She is for now. Or she will be soon. But at the moment, she's answering some questions for us."

"I don't understand."

Clay shook his head. "I'm sorry, man. It's all I can say for now." He started to walk away, then glanced back at Sawyer. "You and Kelsey were talking? I didn't realize you were friends."

They weren't, apparently, judging by her attitude toward him. Though he supposed he hadn't helped matters by failing to recognize her before she gave her name.

Sawyer shook his head, being honest with both himself and Clay. "We're not, really."

"But you didn't mind helping her?"

"Right."

Clay ran a hand through his hair, looked around. "Listen, I know this doesn't make a lot of sense, but something about this doesn't feel right to me. I think they'll let Kelsey go soon and I can't help her because I'm needed here. We've taken everyone's statements and I was just about to announce that everyone's free to go. Do you think you could go to the station and offer to give her a ride, make sure she's okay?"

"Yeah, I can do that." It beat wandering around here in a suit, trying to stay calm, like one of the band members on the Titanic while it went down. "Are you two dating?"

Clay laughed. "Her mom and my mom are sisters. I'd say that's a no."

Cousins. How had he missed that in high school? That shouldn't have made Sawyer as relieved as it did. He didn't remember ever being attracted to Kelsey in high school, though he'd admired her intellect and competitive spirit. Was he that shallow that the fact that she'd grown up gorgeous had made her catch his attention? Or had he just changed enough to recognize that Kelsey Jackson might be a special kind of woman?

"I'll go see what I can do," Sawyer said, and Clay nodded.

"Thanks, man."

Then the other man was gone, leaving Sawyer to jog toward his truck and wonder how this night that had started out as an obligation—a somewhat boring one, at that—had turned into some kind of secret mission to make sure a woman who couldn't stand him was all right, safe from a threat Sawyer didn't yet understand.

Kelsey sat in the small room that passed for an interrogation room in Treasure Point. Really, it was an old office that the officers usually used as a sort of lounge. It was where the coffeepot was, and the smell of burnt coffee filled her nose and made her ready to confess anything just so she could get out of this room, out of this town and back to her life in Savannah.

Except sheer stubbornness meant that she wasn't about to confess when she wasn't guilty of anything. Quite the opposite, she was one of the most promising witnesses they had. So why this treatment? They'd kept her waiting in here for nearly an hour.

The door squeaked as it began to open. Kelsey braced herself. As boring as it had been to sit here, and as eager as she was to get this over with so she could leave, she was not looking forward to any line of questioning that pointed to her as a murderer, a concept so atrocious to her she couldn't let her mind dwell on it.

But instead of Davies's smirk, ready for an interrogation, it was the chief's weathered, familiar face.

"Sir! What are you doing here?"

He cracked the smallest of smiles behind his facial hair. "I work here. Although I could ask the same of you."

Kelsey looked down.

"Listen, I talked to the lieutenant. And I've been over to the museum to see where all of this happened, and I talked to Clay Hitchcock. Let's start this over, shall we?"

"How so?"

"It sounds like you have some useful information about Michael Wingate's murder."

Murder. Kelsey shivered.

"But I'm not looking at you as a suspect. This town and this department has had enough *foh-paaahs* lately."

She tamped down the giggle that his overly Southern pronunciation of *faux pas* had brought on.

"Tell me what you saw, Kelsey." He pulled out the chair across from her. Leaned back.

Kelsey weighed her options. She could still ask for a lawyer and refuse to answer any questions until counsel arrived. She was taking a chance sharing everything she knew. If someone was eager to frame her, they could twist the information she gave against her.

But she knew from her time on the force that the chief was a man of honor. She wouldn't end up locked up without a cause, and the best thing she could do was give him the story he was asking her for, just in case any of it helped. Besides, the information would clear her name for good in case anyone was wondering. The balcony should show signs of a struggle between a pair of people much larger than she was. They might even get footprints that clearly didn't match her heels, or other pieces of physical evidence like hairs or fibers.

"I needed some air." Kelsey began, and she told the chief about leaving the main party area, finding a darkened room, then hearing voices and the sounds of a struggle.

"I went straight to Clay and told him and he went out to investigate. The next thing I knew, the lights were off."

"The lights?"

"All of them, sir. Someone flipped a breaker, I would guess. But what I want to know is why? It's not as if the murderer needed to sneak up on Mr. Wingate. The murder had already taken place. And if the darkness was to cover his escape, why bother? The museum has multiple exits. Even if he looked as though he'd been in a struggle, it would have been easy enough for him to sneak away without being seen after the body fell. Why draw attention to the fact that something was going on when he had the chance for a clean getaway?"

"Maybe he panicked?"

She shook her head slowly. "I don't think so. Something about this feels cold-blooded to me. I don't think it was premeditated, but I don't think the pushing was an accident. I do think whoever the other man was, he meant to kill Wingate."

"Solid reason for that?"

"No. Just gut instinct."

The chief said nothing to that. She wouldn't have expected him to—no words were necessary to remind her that her gut instinct had been wrong before. With devastating consequences for her career. In the case that had ended her tenure with the Treasure Point police department, she'd had a pair of conflicting statements to reconcile regarding a theft from Sawyer Hamilton's wealthy, influential parents. The senior Hamiltons had pointed fingers at a former employee of theirs, a man named Scott Nicholson.

Given her own grudge against Sawyer, it hadn't taken much for Kelsey to feel sympathy for Nicholson, a man from humble beginnings who seemed to be suffering from the Hamiltons' prejudice. Believing in his innocence, she chose to release him from custody, not knowing that they'd find ironclad evidence against him just a few hours later. Her bad judgment meant that he almost managed to escape punishment entirely—they barely managed to catch him before he fled town.

"So, where do we go from here?" Kelsey spoke up,

recognizing that she did so because the silence made her uncomfortable. Too much silence gave her time to think about the past, something she preferred to avoid.

"From here, you're free to go. I only wanted your testimony. Davies was being a bit overzealous for justice in this case. He could have taken your statement at the scene. Bringing you down here in the back of the squad car was unnecessary." He shook his head. "I'm sorry about that."

"Thank you."

Kelsey rose to her feet and preceded the chief out of the office. She'd just turned back to him to ask about a ride when he motioned ahead of her and said "Watch out." But it was one second too late.

This time she didn't see the person she ran into. But the odd sense of déjà vu—mixed with the smell of his woodsy cologne—confirmed there was a good chance it was…

"Sawyer Hamilton. Good to see you." The chief stuck a hand past Kelsey. She was more than happy to step out of the way.

Everything about taking this job had thrown her off balance—literally, it seemed. Clearly staying away from the young heir to the Hamilton name and all it entailed was her only option to regain her equilibrium. Which suited Kelsey just fine.

"Did you need to see me?" the chief asked when Sawyer offered no explanation for why he was there.

The other man's eyes darted to Kelsey. She looked away. Why was he looking at her?

"No, sir, I actually came to check on Kelsey. I heard she was here and thought she might need a ride home."

She'd rather walk the four miles to her family's old

farmhouse on the edge of town than accept. Four miles in the dark in heels and a dress would be preferable to—

"That's very kind of you, Sawyer." The chief had softened his voice to what Kelsey had used to refer to as his "fatherly" tone. He looked over at her. "I would feel better if you accepted his offer."

What, could he read her mind?

Unfortunately, it often seemed like the answer was yes. And he'd always been kind to her, even when most in the department had written her off as a failure and a fool. Which meant that while there was a large group of people Kelsey would mouth off to in this situation without hesitation, and then do what she wanted—trek home in the dark—she couldn't do that to the chief. She owed him better than that.

"I will, sir," she said, forcing herself to turn to face the last man on earth she wanted anything to do with. "I'd appreciate a ride." She forced the words out.

"I'm right out front."

Without a backward glance, Kelsey followed him down the hall and outside. Might as well get this over with.

THREE

The F-150 wasn't what she would have guessed Sawyer Hamilton would drive. Sure, it was a nice truck, but it was the same exact one he'd driven in high school. She'd have assumed he'd moved on by now, maybe to a new BMW or something more like that.

He walked around to the passenger side and opened the door for her. She raised an eyebrow. "Uh, thanks?"

He just laughed softly, a laugh that some women—*most* women—might have thought was endearing. "You're welcome. I haven't been gone from Treasure Point so long, Kelsey, that I forgot how I was raised."

Another reminder that he was still a Hamilton—one of the *haves* when she was a *have not*. And while he hadn't played any role in the fiasco where she'd lost her job, he was the man who'd chosen to compete for a scholarship he didn't need, who'd stolen her chance to go right to college, finish in four years, and get her career moving when all of her peers had.

No, instead she'd stayed in Treasure Point, worked at the police department while she struggled to put herself though school, and now was *just* beginning to see the fruits of her labor, was *just* now approaching where she wanted to be in life.

Kelsey glared at him as he shut her door, walked around to the other side of the truck, then climbed in.

He'd barely sat down when she stopped in the middle of fastening her seatbelt. Loyalty to the chief only went so far. She wasn't doing this to herself. "You know what? I'd actually like the walk. Thanks, though." She reached for the door handle, but his voice stopped her.

"What problem do you have with me, Kelsey? I haven't seen you in a decade, so I assume it must have been something in school, but I always thought we were... I don't know, friendly rivals? Maybe even friends?"

What did it say about him that he'd counted her as a friend? She never, *never* would have thought the same about him.

Either way, his reminder about how much time had passed stilled her. She was an adult now. Close to successful. So far from that bitter, angry seventeen-year-old kid. Surely she could be mature, not let him get to her, right?

"Fine."

He put the car in Reverse and maneuvered his way out of the parking lot. "Are you in the same house you were in during high school?" he asked and at her nod, he headed in that direction.

"Oh, wait, my car. It's at the museum. Could we swing by there?"

"Sure."

He turned around in an empty parking lot and drove back in the direction of the museum. Neither spoke for a minute, and Kelsey wanted to keep it that way, but one thing was bothering her enough that she was willing to break her "say nothing" rule.

"How did you know I was at the police station?" She

braced herself as she asked the question. Had everyone seen her getting ushered into the back of the police car? She hoped not, but if so, better to know now so she could call her boss and do damage control with her job before the situation sounded worse than it was.

"I was talking to Clay. He said you might need a lift."

"That's all he said?" She cast a quick glance at him, meant to look away and didn't.

Sawyer's eyes never left the road, but he nodded. "That's all he said."

Kelsey studied him for another minute. He'd grown up since high school, something that should have been obvious, but that hadn't struck her till now. He still had that confident look of a guy used to winning at everything, but his shoulders had broadened, his jaw-line grown even stronger. The combination should have made him look even more arrogant. And yet...

If she looked closely, a bit of the cockiness was gone. He seemed a little less intimidating than he'd always been.

Intimidating? Did she just admit she'd been intimidated by him? As they drove down the dark road, making the last few turns before the Hamilton property, she realized that yes, she had been. That didn't mean she'd backed down from academic competition with him—that was far from the truth. But maybe her dislike of him had been rooted partly in her own insecurity?

That and his part in ruining her life. She couldn't forget that.

It looked like most of the party had cleared out of the museum, something Kelsey knew the police department would have orchestrated. From what Sawyer had said—or rather, *hadn't* said—the public didn't know about the murder yet. The police officers would have taken everyone's statements, but would have given as little information as possible, not wanting to bias or influence anyone's recollections. And now that everyone was gone, they'd be hard at work establishing a perimeter around the crime scene, so they could begin their investigation.

It was funny how much Kelsey wished she was out there with them, checking for evidence, processing the scene. Police work had just been a practical fallback when her dreams of leaving town for college had come crashing down. But to her surprise, it had become something she'd enjoyed. Who knew the desire to investigate was still so strong inside her?

"There's my car." Kelsey motioned to the dark blue Jeep Patriot.

Wordlessly, Sawyer pulled his truck in beside it. "It really was good to see you again, I wasn't just saying that. Take care of yourself, okay?"

"Yeah," Kelsey replied instinctively, too startled to formulate many thoughts. Take care of herself? Why would he say that like he cared? "Uh, you, too." She scrambled out of the truck as gracefully as she could and shut the door, breathing a sigh of relief as she did so. Hopefully their paths wouldn't cross again while she was still in town and she wouldn't have to examine her own attitudes toward him anymore. Those feelings were one large tangle of confusion. And Kelsey disliked confusion.

Careful to stay mostly on her toes and not sink her silver heels into the dirt to avoid rolling an ankle, she walked the few steps to her car carefully and reached for the door handle.

But…there on the windshield.

What was that?

As every alarm in her mind blared, she reached for the white rectangle, opened the envelope, which wasn't sealed but just folded shut, and pulled a slip of paper out of it.

Typed. Naturally. No need to leave more evidence than necessary.

On autopilot, she unfolded the crisp white paper, folded precisely into three sections.

She read the words she'd somehow known were coming.

YOU HAVE TWELVE HOURS TO GET OUT OF TREASURE POINT. BE GONE BY TO-MORROW MORNING OR FACE THE CON-SEQUENCES. PS I'M WATCHING YOU. CAN YOU SEE ME?

Sawyer had been raised to be a gentleman. No matter how cold Kelsey had been to him, he was going to sit right here in this pickup and wait until she'd climbed into her car and safely driven away. Something had happened in Treasure Point tonight, something dangerous. While he might not know what it was, Kelsey's strange behavior and her presence at the police department—not in an official capacity, it seemed—pointed to her being involved, and possibly in danger, one way or another.

Somehow he felt even more responsible for her safety than he would have another woman. Maybe it was the knowledge that he'd gotten the scholarship she'd wanted—a pretty stupid thing to be trying to make up for a decade later. Especially since she probably didn't remember, and how could she blame him? He'd had dreams to pursue, too, dreams his father hadn't necessarily approved of and had told him in no uncertain terms he wouldn't finance. So he'd worked like crazy on that speech, won the competition and double majored in business—his father's dream for him—and marine biology—his dream for himself, one he never would have been able to reach without that scholarship. There had been other scholarships, but this one had covered nearly all the tuition. He hadn't wanted to alienate his father by dropping the business degree altogether... And the fact was that while he'd gotten the marine biology degree, he hadn't used it yet, hadn't wanted to face the drama that was sure to come if he left the family business altogether.

He saw her reach for the car door and put his truck in Drive, keeping his foot on the brake. He didn't like how all this made him feel, didn't like revisiting the past. From his perspective, it had been a good past, sure, but something about it obviously bothered Kelsey, and he wasn't much for analyzing things that had happened years before. Time to let it go, maybe time for him to let his guilt go over that scholarship money, then both of them could move on. It was clear she didn't want anything to do with him.

Coming back to Treasure Point, being the official representative of the Hamilton family at this museum shindig and all the other official museum events coming up in the next month, was one of the ways he was earning his redemption for the business mistakes he'd had hanging over his head for the last year, ever since the project he'd taken a gamble on had come crashing down—along with most of his father's respect for him. Doing this well was one way to earn that back, which was why he hadn't protested much when the opportunity was offered to him. Aunt Mary couldn't do it because her health was declining, and his parents had other obligations. That and Sawyer suspected that while they enjoyed their prominent position in the town, they viewed actually participating in town events to be somewhat beneath them. In any case, he was happy to do it in their place. He'd officially taken a month of paid vacation time from his father's company, but unofficially, Sawyer was fairly certain he was through trying to make himself fit in a world where he didn't belong. Marine biology had been his passion—here was his chance to look for a job where he could use those skills. The family obligations had provided a good excuse to take this vacation, a plus in his mind. He hadn't anticipated that it would also give him the chance to make the past up to Kelsey, as well. Or at least try to, if she would let him.

She didn't seem to want his regret, didn't need his friendship. And Sawyer refused to sit around and let that nag at him.

Foot raised over the gas pedal, he looked at Kelsey again. Why was it taking her so long to get into the car?

Something about this wasn't sitting well in his stomach. Slowly, he lowered his foot back to the floor and put the truck back into Park, almost in slow motion.

Was that something in her hands? What was she doing?

Kelsey looked over her shoulder first, then spun in his direction, eyes wide. She looked back at her car.

He rolled down the passenger side window. "You need something?"

"No." She said it firmly, cutting him off before the whole sentence had even tumbled from his mouth. But he wouldn't let her push him away that easily.

"Look, whatever you think of me, I'm not stupid. I can tell something's wrong, Kelsey. Maybe you should get back in my truck."

She turned toward him, eyes flashing. But no sound left her mouth. Neither of them had a chance to say anything before a sharp crack, like a firecracker, but with more weight, split the air.

"Get down!" he yelled, but she'd already dropped by the time he said it. Had she been downed by the gunshot or were her instincts that fast?

He was just about to push his own door open, run out there and see if she was all right when the passenger door opened and she jumped in.

Another shot rang out, just as she was climbing in. This one hit metal.

"Go!" Kelsey yelled. He was already working on it. He peeled out, tires squealing like they hadn't since he was sixteen, and drove. He didn't ease up on the gas till they were mostly down the drive that led out of the Hamilton estate and back to the main road.

Kelsey had pulled out her phone and had it lifted to her ear. He needed an explanation, wanted to know especially why she seemed to calm, so unsurprised by this. But he imagined she was probably calling the police, and that was more important right now.

He heard someone on the other end answer. The voice was low. Male. The chief?

"This is Kelsey. You need to know that somebody wants me dead."

She said it calmly. Like it was a fact, nothing more, no feelings attached.

Someone wanted her dead. Why? Was it connected to whatever had happened at the museum? What had she gotten mixed up in? Uncertainty clouded the edges of his judgment. What did he really know about Kelsey Jackson? Nothing. And hadn't he heard rumors here and there—he tried not to pay attention to small-town gossip, but it was impossible to avoid altogether—that she hadn't left the police department on the best terms?

She set the phone down. He glanced over at her. "Where are we going?" He kept his own voice calm and measured. The chief seemed to trust her; that had to be enough for him now. He couldn't exactly leave her on the side of the road when someone had been shooting at her ninety seconds before.

"I'm not sure yet."

"What *are* you sure of?" he asked as he kept driving. He'd grown up here, knew every back road in a thirty-mile radius, minimum, and he had a full tank of gas. If driving was what she wanted, that's what they'd do.

She looked over at him. "You really didn't hear anything about what happened tonight?"

He shrugged. "It's pretty clear that *something* happened, but the police were being pretty closemouthed about it all." Sawyer glanced over at her, but nothing in her expression gave away any of her thoughts. She must have been one impressive cop. He turned back to the road. "Was something vandalized?" he guessed. "Or stolen?" A theft would explain the police response, but not the gunshots. What had she done that resulted in someone wanting her dead?

"Not as far as I know. But Michael Wingate is dead."

"The curator?" The man had been around Treasure Point for as long as Sawyer could remember, but their paths hadn't crossed much when he was a kid—he'd guess Michael was about twenty, maybe thirty years older. He'd met him formally for the first time yesterday.

"Someone pushed him off a balcony. I overheard it happening just a few minutes before the lights went out. Now someone wants me dead."

"What was on your car that made you stop?"

"A note." Kelsey looked down at her lap, leaned over to look at the floor. "I must have dropped it during the shooting. It said I had twelve hours to get out of town or I'd pay for it, basically."

"They didn't give you until morning, though."

She shook her head. "No. I don't know why."

"Maybe the note was a trap itself, just to get you to stand in one place."

"Could be. Who knows?"

Sawyer kept driving, winding his way through the tall pine trees that towered over the darkened back roads.

Kelsey said nothing. He got the feeling she was still deciding whether or not she could trust him.

And Sawyer was trying to decide the same thing. One thing was certain, though. He wasn't going to be able to drive away and put the dangers of Kelsey's situation behind him.

FOUR

She'd been in Treasure Point for less than forty-eight hours, and Kelsey was already on her second trip to the police station. At least this time, she was in the chief's office, waiting for him to come back in.

"Just can't stay away, can you?" one of the officers teased as he walked by the room. Kelsey offered a small smile back, thankful the teasing seemed to be good-natured.

Lieutenant Davies strolled through the door, piercing her with a hard glare. "It seems you're a regular magnet for trouble, huh, Jackson?"

He'd always called her by her last name. He didn't consistently do that to any of the male officers and it had always rankled her.

But he was one man who'd never intimidated her. "No, it just seems that this town isn't the sweet little hamlet by the sea that some people like to pretend that it is."

He studied her for a minute. "That's what you're going with? You don't think it looks oddly coincidental to us that years ago you were in a relationship with a suspect *while* you were an officer, aided him in getting away with the crimes he committed, and now you're back and there's trouble at the museum?"

"I wasn't in a relationship with a suspect." Kelsey took a deep breath, pushed back memories of the past, and kept talking. She'd let a guilty man go because she'd misjudged him, that was it. How had the rumor mill managed to morph the story from the truth to something so salacious was beyond her. "I looked up all the information on the museum before I took the job here, Lieutenant. I'm well aware that there's been trouble at the museum since the idea was barely a spark in the historical society's eye." The museum had suffered several bouts of sabotage in a failed attempt to avoid the discovery of a years-old murder victim on the grounds.

Davies had nothing to say to that. Keeping quiet, he set down a stack of manila envelopes on the table, took a seat at the chair opposite her and stared.

The chief walked in just then. "Kelsey, I've got almost all my men at the museum—they're collecting evidence on Mr. Wingate's death, but they also started looking for any clues as to your attacker as soon as they heard the shots fired." He turned to Davies. "I actually need you back there now, supervising."

The lieutenant walked out without another word to Kelsey, which was fine with her.

Although facing the chief when he was wearing his current expression was a bit intimidating.

"What's going on here?" he asked.

"I don't know, sir."

"You believe you witnessed a murder tonight."

"Yes."

"We don't have any evidence of foul play yet, nothing except your testimony to tell us it was anything other than an accidental death." The older man shook his head.

"It'd be likely this won't be treated as a murder, except that we went through a similar case recently. Because of that we will treat this one as though it is a homicide, whether preliminary evidence supports that or not."

Kelsey let out a breath. At least she could let go of the worry that the department wouldn't take this seriously.

"Did you see anything that could help us find the person responsible?"

"Just dark shapes. I heard more than I saw. As soon as I walked into that room I knew something wasn't right. There was just a feeling…" She shook her head. "I guess that sounds ridiculous. There was no concrete reason to check things out any further, and yet I couldn't stop myself."

"It's called following your instincts, Kelsey. It's what made you such a good officer."

She snorted.

"That last case doesn't define you. Overall, you did good work here. Sure you don't want to come back?"

Not an option, not for any reason. The dream she'd worked so hard for was within her reach now, and it was a sure thing. She wasn't going back to a world of guesses and suspicions when she had certainty in her new job, that and an opportunity to see the world outside of Treasure Point.

"All right, I know when to give up." The chief cleared his throat. "So you heard a scuffle. You're sure you didn't see anything specific?"

"Just shapes, sir. I could tell someone was pushed off the balcony, but I couldn't make out any identifying features of either of the people."

"We've got Shiloh there now trying to get prints from the crime scene. Maybe we'll catch a break and she'll find something right away."

"Maybe," Kelsey echoed, but she knew that as valuable as forensic evidence was, if the criminal had been extremely careful, there might not be much. Besides, there had been a number of people in and around the museum in the past few days, setting up for the event. The evidence would be difficult to find.

"As for where we go from here...tell me about what happened when you returned to the museum."

She described the note she had found on the windshield, and the shots that had been fired shortly after. She even, grudgingly, shared Sawyer's theory that the note might have been a ploy just to get her to stand still. She didn't like the man, but she couldn't deny that the suggestion made sense.

"If someone is trying to kill you, we need to take that seriously," the chief said when she had finished.

"Sir, you know I'm capable of defending myself."

The chief folded his arms across his barrel chest and leaned back in his chair. "You still have your Georgia concealed carry permit, right?"

"Yes, sir."

"And a weapon?"

"Not on me." Something she'd regretted most of the evening, but where was she supposed to put a holster when she was wearing a semiformal dress? Kelsey knew it could be done, but figuring out the logistics when she was a private citizen going to a party where she'd had no reason to expect trouble hadn't been a high priority.

"Locked up at home?"

She nodded.

"Fix that. Keep it on you at all times when you go out."

"Yes, sir."

He was quiet for a minute, and maybe Kelsey was

out of line in asking what she was about to ask, but she was tired, hungry and felt oddly chilled even though she wasn't cold at all. The night was hot and sticky, like any June night in Treasure Point. "Is there anything else, sir?"

The chief's heavy eyebrows did raise in surprise, but she didn't see any judgment or anger in his eyes at her abrupt question. He'd always been very understanding.

"That's all for tonight."

Kelsey stood and walked toward the door.

"One more thing."

She turned back to her old boss. "Yes?"

"Is that Hamilton boy still here?"

She laughed a little at his description. The chief was well into his sixties, though, so it made sense he'd refer to Sawyer that way.

"He's waiting around here somewhere," Kelsey admitted.

"If he'll take you home, take him up on it. It's less likely anyone will try something if there are two of you."

"There were two of us when I was shot at."

"I know, Kelsey, but I can't spare anyone for a protection detail right now, so this is the best I can do."

"I'll ask him," she conceded, mostly because the chief was looking at her with that protective look on his face that she recognized from her time on the force. He was a man who was never okay with one of his own getting hurt, and sexist or not, he had always seemed to be even more careful with Kelsey and Shiloh, the only two woman officers. Kelsey was afraid if she didn't agree to ask Sawyer, the chief himself would insist on giving her a ride home.

"You do that. Good night, Kelsey. Stay safe."

She nodded, then moved away from his door. She'd

barely made it out of that hallway into the main area of the building when she spotted Sawyer. She'd half hoped he'd gone and she could find another ride, but that was apparently too much to wish for.

"Ready to go home?" he asked her.

Actually, it was about the last thing she was ready for. But she didn't have many other options, because while running from this town, this situation, might seem unbearably tempting, it also wasn't an option. Her job, her dreams, her life *away from here* depended on her sticking this out, finishing the work she'd come here to do.

"I'm ready." She tried to sound convincing.

Thankfully, Sawyer didn't seem to notice everything she wasn't saying. Like the fact that she wasn't really ready at all. The fact that she was scared.

And the fact that facing Treasure Point again, after all that had happened, was almost as scary as someone wanting her dead.

Sawyer had only just dropped Kelsey off when he heard the screams.

He turned the truck off, threw the door open and ran to where she was standing on the front porch.

"What?"

"I, uh, I thought I saw a spider."

"You didn't." Sawyer didn't believe that for a second.

"I really did. He went back in that corner."

She motioned to a darkened corner of the porch filled with who knew what. "What is all that?" She'd always seemed so organized and attentive to little details, he was surprised she was able to live here with that mess.

"I'm not sure."

"This *is* your house, right?"

"My parents' house."

"Where are they?"

"They moved to Savannah when I finished high school. They've been renting the house, but the last renters did a number on the place, as you can see, so my folks want to sell it and get out of the landlord business."

Sawyer couldn't stop the raising of his eyebrows. "And they're going to sell it like this?"

"No, of course not. When I told them I would be working in the area for a few weeks, they asked if I'd start getting the place cleaned up while I was here."

He took in the chipping blue paint—really, blue?—the unidentified mess in the corner and the general disrepair of the place. There was nothing structurally unsound as far as he could tell. It wasn't in awful condition. But it wasn't in great shape to sell, either. *That* he did know something about since, as his dad always said, "Hamiltons know real estate, son." He decided not to comment on it, changing the subject instead. "So, what are you doing in town? You never said."

She explained about her insurance job and the work she was doing with the museum. "I've got an assignment lined up in St. Simons next, so I'll be staying in town for that, too."

He nodded. "That explains why you were at the museum tonight—but not why someone was shooting at you. Or what happened to make you scream just now, because I know you don't expect me to believe it was a spider."

"I really did think I saw one."

Something about the way she said that...

"Is that all?"

"No. And if you're going to ask me what it was, you may as well come in. I didn't get to eat much at the party and I'm starving."

"You're cooking?"

"If you consider bologna sandwiches cooking, then yes."

"Any chance I could get one of those?"

Kelsey's snort of laughter wasn't quite ladylike, but it was cute when she did it. She shook her head as she stuck her key in the doorknob and pushed the door open. "Sawyer Hamilton eats bologna?"

"Why wouldn't I?" He followed her inside, noting that the inside of the house was in better condition than the outside. That made him feel better about her staying here.

"You're a *Hamilton*."

"Who still has to eat to stay alive."

"But bologna is such…such peasant food."

The ridiculousness of this conversation was getting to him. At least, that's the only excuse Sawyer could formulate for what he did next. He reached for Kelsey's hand, laid it on top of his own palm and brushed her fingers over the calluses on his fingers and palm.

Their eyes met. Held. Sawyer swallowed hard. He hadn't expected touching her to focus all his senses quite this way, narrow his gaze to where he only saw her. Her green eyes. Staring right at him.

He dropped her hand, tried to recover his composure. "Those are a working man's hands, Kelsey. When I'm not at work, I'm outside, doing things in the yard, working with my hands as much as I can. I guess I'm just a 'peasant' like you. Now, how about that bologna while you tell me what really had you spooked?"

She locked the front door behind them and nodded. "Okay, give me one minute." And she ran up the stairs.

Not two minutes later she was back, dressed in jeans and a sleeveless button-down shirt. He couldn't blame her. He was suffocating in his suit. He tugged at his tie, rolled it up and put it in his suit pocket, then slid out of the jacket. "Good idea with the clothes."

"Yeah, I don't stay dressed up any longer than I have to. Besides, I needed my gun."

He didn't see any gun.

Kelsey grinned, patted her hip. "It's a good concealment holster. I got my permit as soon as I wasn't law enforcement anymore. I let the cops do their job and I'm not out to be a vigilante with it, but as far as protecting myself goes, I'd prefer to be able to."

Sawyer nodded. It was a common attitude in the South, and one that gave him great relief when it came to Kelsey's safety.

"So, tell me why you really screamed." He finally brought the subject back to the one she'd managed to dance gracefully away from two different times now.

"Any chance you'll just let it go?"

"Nope."

"Fine. There was another note on the door."

"And you just stood there? Didn't the shooter use a note earlier to get you to stay in one place so they could shoot at you?"

"Possibly—we can't really say for sure that that was his method the first time. At any rate, he obviously didn't shoot at me this time."

"What did the note say?"

"Basically the same as the other." She reached into her pocket and pulled out a crinkled piece of paper. "I balled it up after I read it and held it in my fist while you and I were talking."

Back when she'd been trying to convince him that she'd been scared enough of a spider to scream. Sure.

Sawyer took the note she was offering.

YOU SEEM TO HAVE A HARD TIME LISTENING. THOSE SHOTS WERE WARNING SHOTS, SO YOU'D KNOW TO TAKE THE NOTE SERIOUSLY. YOU HAVE UNTIL SEVEN TOMORROW. NO ONE ELSE HAS TO DIE.

BUT IF YOU CHOOSE NOT TO LISTEN… YOU WILL.

"This is why you screamed?"

She shook her head. Reached into her pocket again. "I bagged it as soon as I took it upstairs." She slid a paper bag out of her pocket and reached inside.

And pulled out a picture printed on computer paper. It was a picture of Kelsey, from tonight at the museum event. And it was marked through with something red. And sticky.

"That's not real blood, right?"

She shook her head. "I don't think so. But I called the police when I was upstairs. They're sending a couple of officers over to retrieve it and process the outside of my house for any trace evidence left on the porch."

Sawyer took it all in, absorbed the way she said it all, so matter-of-factly and full of confidence. Kelsey had been smart in high school. Quick-witted. But he didn't remember her being this sure of herself.

"I'm glad you called them."

"Of course I did. I wouldn't try to handle this myself…" But her voice trailed off in a funny way, like that was exactly what she was considering doing.

She'd always been independent—he remembered that from school. He also remembered the way it had isolated her, keeping her from being really close to anyone. She'd only ever had casual friends. He doubted she'd kept up with much of anyone from high school…

which meant there was no one in Treasure Point for her to lean on for support now, especially with her parents no longer living in town.

Sure, there was her cousin, Clay, but he'd be focused on police work, logging evidence and following procedure. If Kelsey did any investigating on her own, Clay wouldn't be able to help her. So who did that leave?

Me.

The idea was crazy, but there was no question in Sawyer's mind that Kelsey Jackson was in danger, and she didn't need to face this on her own, even if that was how she was used to doing life. Sawyer had to be in Treasure Point, anyway, to be the face of his family at the events surrounding the museum's opening.

When he wasn't doing that...

He may as well be talking Kelsey into letting him tag along wherever she was going. Not that he didn't think she could handle herself, but maybe he'd serve as a good distraction while she shot at the bad guys.

In any case, he was going to stick to her like glue, whether she liked it or not.

Sawyer was pretty sure it was going to be "not."

FIVE

She dreamed about the gunshots that night, and woke with a feeling of pressure on her chest that made it hard to breathe, almost like a physical weight that reminded her of the truth that weighed on her mind—someone had threated to kill her. He'd made it clear that he would make good on those threats if she wouldn't be bullied into leaving.

And Kelsey had no intention of going anywhere. If she left town with her work undone, she'd lose her job. Not to mention, she'd lose her self-respect if she let this town make her run away again. Logically, she knew that leaving would be the smart choice…but she couldn't bring herself to do it.

Which meant today, tomorrow, as many days as this took…things were only going to get worse.

She climbed out of her car—the officers had processed it for evidence and then Clay had brought it home for her—after parking in front of the museum, and stopped to look up when she heard a noise. Her whole body tensed, ready to run or fight or whatever she needed to do. She put her hand on her hip where she could feel the reassuring lump of the gun concealed inside her waistband.

But there was no need for alarm. It was a truck pulling into the parking lot, one she recognized immediately from all the time she'd spent in it last night.

What was Sawyer Hamilton doing here?

She tried not to watch him as he parked the truck and stepped out, but like it or not, her eyes were drawn to him. He reached back into the truck for something. Sawyer stepped back out with coffee.

"What are you doing here?" She voiced the question that she hadn't stopped mentally asking since she saw him.

"I figured you'd be here and thought you might have had a rough night."

She stared, understanding not dawning until he reached out with the coffee cup. That was for her?

"You used to get cappuccinos in high school. I hope that's still okay."

"In high school?" She reached for the coffee, feeling like she could use the caffeine to get her out of this fog that seemed to have descended with Sawyer's presence. This concern for her was the last thing she would have expected from him.

"Thank you," she said, allowing herself a small smile. "And cappuccinos...yes, that's still my favorite." They hadn't spent time together outside of their classes in high school that she could remember. Ever. So how had he...?

"I saw you order it more than once when you'd study at the bookstore."

The old bookstore had been the only place to get coffee in Treasure Point all those years ago, and the fancy espresso machine had only lasted five years or so before the owners of the bookstore had sold it, since it wasn't making them much of a profit. At the time, Treasure Point—with the exception of Kelsey—seemed to prefer its coffee plain. It was only recently, when Claire Phillips had returned to town after college, that more people had accepted the idea of "fancy" coffee.

"Well…thanks, then," she repeated, then shook her head and took a long sip of that cappuccino. She closed her eyes for a second. So good.

Unfortunately, after a second, Kelsey acknowledged she had to open her eyes and get to work.

She turned away from Sawyer and walked toward the front door of the museum. She'd been scheduled to work with Michael Wingate. With him dead… Kelsey wasn't sure how this was supposed to work anymore. The rules had changed. Would she even be allowed to work today, or was the museum still being treated as a crime scene?

The door of the museum opened just then, and a dark-haired woman stepped out. Gemma O'Dell, the marketing manager for the museum. Kelsey had met with her briefly when she'd first arrived back in town.

"Kelsey, you came."

"Were you doubting that I would?"

"We weren't sure with…" she shot a glance at the two police cars parked at the edge of the lot "…with everything that happened yesterday," she finished. "Matt almost didn't let me come to work today." She said the last part with a grin and Kelsey knew she didn't really mind the overprotectiveness of her husband, Matt O'Dell.

"So, will I be working with you today?"

Gemma shook her head and moved her hand to the baby bump that was quite obvious. "Even though I don't officially go on maternity leave until the baby comes—"

"You're due any day?" Kelsey guessed. She didn't have much experience with babies or childbirth, but she was fairly certain that Gemma's stomach had no more room for expansion, so she figured it must be close.

Gemma nodded. "Yes, and Matt wants me to do as much work from home as I can these last couple of weeks. Or days. I'm voting days."

Kelsey laughed. "I'm sure you are."

"Anyway, especially with the murder, here at the museum is not somewhere he wants me spending a lot of time. Not that there's any reason to assume there will be more crimes. You shouldn't be worried."

Oh, if only Gemma knew.

"I'm not going to let it stop me from doing my job," Kelsey reassured the other woman.

"Great. I'll let you get started and I'll be in my office for about an hour. After that, I'm headed home, but you can call me if you need anything. Do you need any help from me, or do you know where to get started today?"

"You can head to your office," Kelsey assured her. "I know where to go and what to do." As exhausted as Gemma looked already, Kelsey was relatively certain she wasn't going to be bothering her. Gemma was one of the few full-time staff members at the museum, which meant that she was in for a day of answering worried phone calls and dealing with the public response in reaction to the murder. Clearly, she had enough on her plate, and Kelsey wouldn't add to it.

With a relieved smile, Gemma went back inside, heading toward her office. Kelsey started to enter the building as well, but the manners her mother had drilled into her made her turn around to finish her conversation with Sawyer first.

"Are you coming in?" she asked. "Did you have some business with the museum today?"

"No, I just came by to check on you."

Kelsey blinked. "You…what?"

He shrugged, looking uncomfortable but sincere. "I

just came by to check on you," he repeated. "And to make sure you wouldn't be here by yourself, after those threats last night."

That was unexpected. But she tried to brush it off. "I'll be fine," she insisted. She pointed to the cop cars. "I won't be here alone."

"Good—that's good." He looked awkward, as if he had something to say, but wasn't sure how to phrase it. Finally, he blurted out, "Let me know if you're going to be on your own later, okay?"

"Why?"

"So I can come over."

"But *why*?" This wasn't making any sense. "You don't have to look after me. I'm not your responsibility, and I can take care of myself."

"You shouldn't have to," he replied, taking the wind right out of her sails. "Dealing with threats and attacks isn't something anyone should have to do on their own. I know the police will do what they can, but they have lots of responsibilities to handle, whereas I'm here in town with time on my hands. I can help. I *want* to help. Will you let me?"

He looked so hopeful that Kelsey couldn't bring herself to say no—it would feel like kicking a puppy. An unwanted puppy who seemed to want nothing more than to get underfoot. So, fine, she'd agree to let him help, and then she'd just conveniently forget to contact him later. Problem solved.

Satisfied with her assurance that she'd let him know when she needed him—which would be at a quarter past never—Kelsey went inside and got to work.

She spent the day wandering the museum, estimating the value of some of the antiques that she could identify easily, and researching others to figure out comparisons that would tell her what they might be worth. She'd done the job before, many times, but always with direct supervision. It was a big vote of confidence from her employer that she was being allowed to do this, as well as another job, on her own.

Kelsey was supposed to spend tomorrow in St. Simons at the estate that was her other large project right now. At first, the Treasure Point Historical Society hadn't been excited at the prospect of her attention being divided, but Kelsey had insisted she could handle both of the jobs. Her boss hadn't given her a choice about the museum job, since the town had asked for her specifically, but the Medlin Estate was something that would advance her career more, and she wasn't giving that up for anything.

Kelsey knew she could do it, but it was still over-whelming to think about, which was why—on her way back into town—she pulled her car into the parking lot that connected to the coastal trail. She exhaled even before she got out, feeling some of the tension leave her shoulders as she thought about running. It was one of the best ways she knew to relieve stress.

She'd changed into running clothes before leaving the museum, so she climbed from her car, set her phone to her running playlist and put it on her armband. Hesitating for a second, she pulled the phone back out for a second and sent a quick text to Sawyer, just to let some-one know where she was. She regretted the message the moment she'd sent it. Sawyer didn't need to know where she was, especially since the day had been quiet and it seemed like maybe…like maybe the threat from last night hadn't been as big as she'd feared.

Then again, Michael Wingate's body was in the McIntosh County morgue right now, so Kelsey knew that wasn't true.

Either way, the text message was sent and Kelsey needed this run, had plenty of things in her brain that needed to be sorted out.

She started out at a comfortable pace and eased into her workout. The first thought her mind landed on was Sawyer. Nope. She wasn't going there. She sped up a little, felt her feet pound the ground a little harder at the thought of the boy-turned-man who'd thrown her so off balance earlier in the day.

No. No matter what, she wasn't going to think of *him* right now.

Instead she thought about work. Had Matt overreacted by keeping Gemma away from the museum for now? Kelsey wanted to say yes, especially since she didn't want to believe she was truly in danger from her work there…but what other reason could someone have for killing Michael Wingate if it wasn't connected to his job?

She pushed herself a little harder. Today had been calm. Boring, even. She'd walked through most of the exhibits, accompanied by an officer. He was a younger guy, not a native of the town, but he seemed nice enough, even if his couldn't-be-more-than-twenty-one-year-old self kept calling her "ma'am." She loved Southern charm and manners, except when they made her feel like she was much older than pushing thirty.

Kelsey had gotten a lot accomplished as far as her insurance job, but where the investigation was concerned, she wished she could have spent time in the room where the murder had taken place. She'd remembered while she was working that Michael had acted strangely around one exhibit in there in particular, like there was something about it that made him uncomfortable. It was the most fascinating exhibit in the museum—there wasn't any doubt about that. Many of the rooms and exhibits focused on Treasure Point's history in general, but this particular exhibit was exclusively geared toward Treasure Point's pirate history. Blackbeard was only one of the many pirates who had loved this corner of the Eastern Seaboard for all its barrier islands, mysterious swamps and places to hide smuggled goods.

It was Treasure Point's little claim to fame, its most valuable asset as a town trying to grow its tourist trade, as well as its greatest liability. The last few years had seen an upswing in crime for many of the reasons pirates had frequented the area years before.

The exhibit was interesting, but she hadn't seen anything in there worth killing over. Most of it talked about shipwrecks that had happened over a hundred years ago.

Who would kill over that?

Kelsey shook her head, picked up the pace a little. She was coming up on the parking lot. One more lap, she told herself, and then she'd jump into the water to cool off, take a swim in her workout clothes—she had a spare towel in her car she could sit on—before heading back to the house to tackle a few cleaning projects there and eat another sandwich for dinner.

She'd had more fun having that impromptu dinner with Sawyer last night than she liked to admit.

Sawyer? Where had that come from?

She ran faster. Enough of that.

The second lap went quickly, and then she was carefully picking her way along the narrow game trail through the woods that led to the beach. Not many people accessed the beach from here, but it had always been a favorite place of hers to swim. The main beach of Treasure Point wasn't very big, and as a result it was usually crowded.

Kelsey liked having this quiet space to herself.

She narrowly avoided some thorns and pushed her way through the last bit of underbrush until she emerged onto a clearer area, where the dirt of the forest gradually gave way to sand. It was a unique area, in general and environmentally, and Kelsey loved everything about it. This was why, though she'd longed for a big city, she'd settled on Savannah rather than somewhere farther like Atlanta, or even Charleston. This place would always be home in a way, and Savannah was the most similar to Treasure Point.

Kelsey waded into the waves, the water felt good against her hot skin after the initial jolt of cold. The waves lapped against her and she let herself float on them, relax with them and even stayed there on her back for a few minutes, looking up at the blue sky dotted with cotton-ball clouds.

The sound of the waves hitting the beach was loud, but the noise relaxed her. After a few minutes of floating she moved upright again, swam a little closer to the shore since she'd drifted. Then she found the two trees in the distance she liked to use as markers for herself and swam a few laps.

Finally, exhausted, she lay on her back again, exhaled the stress of the day into the warm salty air and let herself relax.

Something snatched her arm, jerked her underwater before Kelsey could react, before she could draw in one more long breath of air to sustain her.

She kept her eyes open even though the salty ocean water stung, but her attempts to see her attacker were useless. The water here was far from clear, and though the sun was shining, all she could see were particles and a shape. Definitely human. She struggled, fought to get away, and managed to wrench her arm free before throw-

ing herself toward the shore and kicking with every bit
of strength she had left.

Was that someone on the beach? Did her attacker
have an accomplice?

She kicked harder, moved her arms in the freestyle
motion, only to be jerked backward again by the man—
she was fairly certain that the shape was too large to be
a woman—and pulled back under. This time she'd taken
a breath, so she had more energy to fight.

Still, as she kicked and struggled, she knew that she
didn't have long. She couldn't keep holding her breath,
but to stop trying was to give up and die.

And Kelsey wasn't a quitter. Never had been. Wasn't
about to start now.

"Kelsey!"

She heard the shouts from the beach. Was the person she'd seen someone on her side, not her attacker's?

The knowledge gave her confidence to give this
struggle all she had, and she landed one solid kick to
her opponent's gut.

The pressure on her arm released. She was free.

And he was gone. Untraceable.

Kelsey surfaced and gasped, never as thankful as
she was right now to be able to draw in air. Someone
had tried to drown her. Someone had almost succeeded.

"Kelsey!" The voice came again and this time she
recognized it. It was Sawyer on the beach.

He'd gotten her message. He'd come.

And, like it or not, whatever her past grudges against
him were, he'd saved her life. She owed him a second
chance.

Sawyer hadn't been clear about what he'd encountered
on the beach. All he knew was that Kelsey had been

underwater, then back up, then under for longer than it seemed like someone would stay under intentionally. Though he hadn't seen anyone but her, the way she'd flailed in the water said she'd been fighting someone.

The same person who'd fired warning shots at her last night?

"Kelsey!" he yelled again. He hadn't gone into the water after her since she'd seemed to get free before he'd had a chance, but even though no one seemed to be attacking her now, he knew he'd keep worrying until he could talk to her and make sure she was uninjured.

This time she met his eyes. The fear he saw in hers unnerved him, like he could almost feel it for himself.

Finally, she emerged from the water and he stepped forward to meet her. Her leggings and her bright green tank top were soaked, as was the ponytail she'd pulled her hair back into. Mascara was smudged on her cheeks and she looked…

Brave. That was how she looked to Sawyer right now. Brave.

He watched her draw in a breath, look behind her again and hurry toward him. When she finally reached his side, she stopped.

"Are you okay?"

She shook her head. Then nodded. "I'm not sure. I'm alive, but…"

"But someone tried to kill you again."

She nodded.

Whoever this was meant business. Those notes weren't meant to intimidate, weren't just bluffs. The killer had told her if she didn't leave town he'd kill her. Clearly he meant to follow through on his promise.

"We need to call the police." Sawyer reached out a hand.

Kelsey nodded. "Yes. And they'll want us to stay here so they can ask you questions at the scene. What do you think, should we wait in the car, though?"

"I think we're okay. You don't see anyone out there anymore, do you?"

"No, but that doesn't mean he's not hiding somewhere. I still don't know where he came from, or how long he was watching me before he came after me. He couldn't have known when I'd get in the water, or even that I'd come to this specific spot, so he must have followed me here."

"And you didn't notice anything suspicious?"

She shook her head, frowning. "I should have…but no, I didn't notice a thing." She looked shaky, now that the adrenaline had faded, so he suggested they sit.

Sawyer tried to keep his distance but at the same time not get farther than a couple of feet from her since she was in danger.

Until he noticed her hand was shaking. Then he reached out and took it in his. Squeezed.

She looked at him funny, but didn't let go until they'd reached the edge of the sand nearest to the trees, where a piece of driftwood formed a more secure spot for them to sit than on the open beach.

"I can't believe that just happened," she said. "That it was really real."

"I'm sure. It's crazy."

"I've got to figure out why this is happening."

"I'm sure when the police get here, they'll do the best they can to—"

"No. *I* have to do it."

Sawyer looked at her face, saw in her eyes that she meant it. "Why? You have enough on your plate with the museum job and trying to stay alive, don't you think? Not to mention fixing up your parents' house."

"Look, I respect the officers at the department here just as much as anyone, probably more since I worked with many of them and got along well with them. But this is personal for me. I feel like if I can focus and put some pieces of whatever kind of puzzle this is together, then I have a better chance of figuring out who is behind this than the police department does."

"You know they're going to put every resource they can toward this, Kelsey. It's not like it won't be taken seriously—a man was already been killed and you've been nearly killed twice."

"I'm not saying that I think they won't give it all they've got. But I'm not going to sit around and either ignore the fact that I'm in danger or hide under the blankets while I wait for someone else to take care of it. I have the skills I need to investigate by myself and so that's what I'm going to do. Just a little digging, maybe enough to find something I can pass on to my friends at the police department that might help them. You know they're like most departments, anyway, perpetually short-staffed, so it's not like they couldn't use the help."

He didn't know what to say. He couldn't really argue that she didn't have the right or the ability to look into this herself, but at the same time, the concept of her diving back into investigating—how many years had it been?—with no team behind her didn't sit well with him. He'd decided earlier that he wanted to help her, that he'd give her some backup and support, but that was when he'd assumed that she'd mostly be lying low, acting defensively to protect herself rather than confronting danger head-on.

"I have to try," she insisted.

As he met her eyes this time, he saw how much she meant it, how determined she was.

"Do you want a ride home when we're done here? I'm guessing the police are going to want to check your car to make sure nothing was tampered with."

She blinked, apparently not prepared for him to give up with so little fight.

"Why do you keep trying to help me? I still don't understand why."

Did she really think he'd just stand by and do nothing while she was in danger? She always seemed to assume the worst of him, and he'd never quite understood why. The truth of it was that he had always liked her, always wished they could be friends, but for whatever reason, she'd always seemed to dislike him more than anyone else. He didn't know if she was just that competitive, but what he'd always viewed as a friendly academic competition between them, she'd always seemed to view as a fight to the death. The way she interacted with him had only gotten worse after the scholarship speech contest he'd beaten her in, in their senior year, right before they graduated. But here they were, adults now, and it seemed like Sawyer was being handed a second chance to be her friend.

And he wanted to take it.

"Like I said before, I'm in town without too many daily responsibilities and you need help." Better to let the rest of his motives speak for themselves.

"See, only a Hamilton would be able to say that. The rest of us? We can't afford to sit around with minimal responsibilities and do nothing all day."

She was soaked, had nearly drowned, and the last thing she needed was someone snapping at her—even if she had it coming—Sawyer reminded himself as she flung the stinging words at him. He wouldn't have guessed they would hurt so much, but they did.

"It's not that I'm doing nothing." He started to defend himself, though he didn't know why he was bothering. She had made up her mind about him and his family—lumped them all together, apparently—long ago, but he still had to try to change her opinion of him. "I'm looking for a job right now."

Her eyebrows raised. The lack of respect on her face was too much.

"You know what, never mind," Sawyer said, voice flat. "I don't have to explain myself to you. If you don't want my help then that's your choice, but lashing out at me isn't going to fix anything."

He watched as her facial expression changed, as she looked down, then back up at him with tears shining in her eyes. "You're right. That was awful of me."

"Can you explain why you dislike me so much?" he asked.

She shook her head. "It's nothing. I wasn't fair, and I'm sorry. Thank you for offering to help." She hesitated. "I'm not very good at accepting help."

"I know."

Kelsey looked confused, like she wasn't aware of how much he'd watched her in high school. He'd always found her fascinating, especially since—in contrast to the other girls at school who fawned over him—he hadn't been able to get Kelsey to so much as crack a smile at the jokes he liked to tell. She was serious, competitive and incredibly smart. And she'd never been willing to give him the time of day. She still seemed pretty unenthused about the idea of spending time with him... but she hadn't said no. She'd even apologized for what she'd said. Maybe they could make this work after all.

"So…truce?" he offered, trying to brush off her words for good, ready to start over. He held out a hand.

"Truce." She shook it.

Officers arrived then—Clay and Officer Ryan, according to the other officer's nametag. He must be new in town, Sawyer didn't know him.

"Can you tell us what happened?" Clay asked.

Kelsey shook her head. "Not really. I was swimming and then someone tried to pull me under. I have no idea who."

"Or why?"

She didn't speak for a minute. "I believe it's tied to the murder at the museum. You know I overheard what happened, and while I didn't see enough to be of any help in the investigation officially, the killer has apparently decided it's not safe to leave me alive." She explained about the threatening notes she'd received.

The younger officer's eyes were widening. Apparently he hadn't been briefed yet. He must be the low man on the police force totem pole. Of course, he looked like he was still a teenager—Treasure Point did allow eighteen-year-olds to serve on the police force, unlike some other areas.

"Anything else we need to know?" Clay asked the younger officer, who Sawyer was almost certain now was in training.

The other man just stood with his eyes wide. Clay sighed and continued. "So you didn't see anything that could help?"

"No. I'm assuming it was someone who can scuba dive, since I didn't see anyone get in or out of the water, and he didn't seem to need to come up for air while he was holding me under. Maybe they were waiting for me. But I don't know how he could have known when or where I'd be in the water."

"The scuba diving doesn't exactly narrow it down much in a beachside town," Sawyer commented. "I dive."

Clay raised his eyebrows. "And where were you?"

"Really, Clay?" Kelsey shook her head. "It's not Sawyer."

"I was here," Sawyer answered, "at least, for the end of it. Kelsey had texted me where she'd be and I wanted to make sure she was all right. But unless I figured out how to release Kelsey, get out of the water ahead of her, shed my scuba gear, change into dry clothes and dry my hair all before Kelsey reached the shore, it couldn't have been me."

"And prior to that, where were you this afternoon?" Clay pressed.

"At the library doing some research. The librarian will be able to vouch for me."

Clay nodded and turned back to Kelsey. "We're going to investigate here and make sure there's nothing that could help us. I'll check your car and then we can drop it by your house, if that works for you."

"I appreciate it. Thanks."

"Well, you know that's not really police protocol, but for cousins..." Clay smiled, then continued on in a more serious tone. "I'll go report all this to the chief and write up a report. Kelsey, you be careful. This seems to be escalating quickly."

Unfortunately, Sawyer agreed.

The officers stayed on the beach to search for any signs a suspect might have left behind, but Sawyer didn't hold out much hope that they'd find anything.

"You are welcome to leave, unless you'd like us to walk back with you," Clay called to Kelsey.

She looked at Sawyer.

"What do you want to do?" he asked, assuming she'd take charge like she always did, always had.

"What do you think?"

There it was, a tiny step toward friendship. He considered it for a minute.

"It's a risk to leave without a police escort, but I don't think it's more of a risk than standing here in the open. I don't believe that whoever tried to kill you is still hanging around at all. I think he got out of here the moment he quit attacking you."

"I think so, too. I'm ready to go home, if you don't mind. And yes, I'd love that ride."

They walked across the beach, Kelsey's running shoes squishing water as they grew more and more covered with sand.

"Do you want to borrow my shoes? I know they're too big…" Sawyer felt like he should offer, though he was pretty sure what her response would be.

"I'm fine. But thanks for offering."

They continued the walk into the woods, onto the coastal trail that people used for running. From where the dirt trail met the bigger paved trail, it wasn't far to the parking lot.

"Do you want dinner or anything?" Sawyer asked as he opened her door for her. "We could stop somewhere on the way to your house."

"No, I'm not fit to be seen in public until I take a shower. If you'd just take me home, that would be great."

Neither of them said much on the way. That was fine with Sawyer. The last few days had been a lot for his mind to process, and not just because of the murder at the museum and the danger to Kelsey's life. He'd also been drawn right back into small-town life, something he hadn't expected. Sawyer had assumed once he left the business his dad owned in Savannah, that he'd end up staying in the city but working with a marine biology organization, or possibly moving to South Carolina or Florida. He'd never planned to return to a little town like this one. But instead of chasing him away again, the last few days, the sense of what it was like to have a close community that cared for each other, even in the midst of crazy circumstances like these, had reminded him what he was missing.

They pulled up in front of Kelsey's house after only a few minutes.

"Thanks for the ride."

Kelsey climbed out of his truck and headed inside.

"Bye," he called after her, watching her go.

Sawyer leaned his seat back and got comfortable. He might change his mind later about guarding the house for the night, if he thought about it and decided he was overreacting. But for now? He wasn't going anywhere.

SIX

As hard as Kelsey tried to push thoughts of Sawyer away, he just wouldn't leave her alone. Which was why she wasn't surprised in the least to see his truck still sitting in her driveway an hour after he'd dropped her off.

She shook her head, slipped her flip-flops on, and walked outside. She stopped beside his window and raised her eyebrows.

He rolled the window down but didn't say anything.

"Are you, like, spying on me, Sawyer, or sitting out here as some kind of unarmed security?"

"I'm a Southern boy, Kelsey. I've got the boots, the ball cap and the truck. Who says I'm unarmed?"

He had a point there.

"Well, what are you doing out here? Didn't I tell you earlier that I'd be fine?"

"Sure, but for some reason words don't mean a whole lot to me when I've personally watched you almost get shot and then almost drown in the same twenty-four-hour period."

"*Almost* doesn't really count, Sawyer."

"When we're talking about you dying? I think it counts enough."

The fierceness in his eyes caught her off guard. She

hadn't thought he hated her or anything—no, he'd always seemed perfectly friendly, the animosity between them had always been one-sided—but the idea that he cared enough about her to get that protective look in his eyes, to sit out here in her driveway making sure she was safe…it was sort of sweet.

"So, this is your plan? Wait out here for weeks or months or who knows how long, until this whole thing has resolved?"

"I don't have much of a plan yet." He stopped talking, surveyed her for a minute. "But it would be a lot easier if you'd just let me help you, let me plan with you the best way to give you a little bit of unofficial backup in whatever completely unsanctioned investigation you have going on."

For once, she pushed her instinctive stubbornness aside and considered it. Finally, she nodded. "For now, why don't you at least come in. Want some food?"

"Bologna again?" he teased. It really was one of his favorites, but it also seemed like a good way to lighten up this conversation.

"Nah. I noticed you out here half an hour ago and went ahead and cooked for two."

His stomach chose that moment to growl. "I could use some food."

Inside, they served themselves and sat down, then Kelsey started to talk.

"Listen, I talked to the chief right after everything started happening. He feels fine knowing that I have a handgun and know how to use it."

"That's not going to solve all your problems, Kelsey. Where was your gun this afternoon when you were swimming? They aren't waterproof, so it's not like you were reckless not taking it, but if you want to live as normal a life as possible while this is going on, something's going to have to give. No one can be on guard around the clock. Not without exhausting themselves and losing effectiveness. You need backup, and despite your aversion, I just think it should be me."

She pushed her mashed potatoes around on her plate. "I wouldn't say I have an *aversion* to you."

"Then what? You've made no secret of the fact that there's something about me that makes you angry. The way you've said *Hamilton* like my last name is some kind of bad word to you... We were friends once, I thought. Can't we go back to that?"

"We weren't really friends, Sawyer. We were rivals. There's a difference."

"Friendly rivals."

Something flashed in her eyes. "Right up until..." Then she cut herself off, cleared her throat. "Do you want any more green beans?" She lifted the pot and moved it toward him.

"No, I don't want any more green beans. What I want is for you to tell me what it is I did a decade ago that makes you not want to be friends with me now."

Banging on her door interrupted their conversation. The relief on her face was unmistakable.

They both stood instantly.

"You stay back a little," she cautioned.

"What, to get a good description of the guy if he manages to shoot you when you open the door?"

The look she gave him made it clear that Sawyer wasn't making any forward progress in the can't we be friends department.

Fine, she could handle this. Sawyer stayed back like she'd asked—not so politely—and watched as Kelsey approached the door looking every bit as if she had a law enforcement past. She moved carefully, hand at the hip where he assumed her weapon was concealed. "Who is it?" she asked, in a voice edged with steel.

"It's Lieutenant Davies and the chief."

Kelsey eased the door open and stepped aside so the two men could enter, dropping her hand to her side again since there was no danger.

"Did you find anything out?"

"Nothing helpful," Davies said, looking to the chief.

The chief continued. "As you probably guessed, there were no witnesses near that stretch of beach, besides Sawyer who we know didn't see anything. You might want to reconsider your jogging route."

"I'll remember that," Kelsey said. Sawyer noted she didn't even come close to agreeing. He made a mental note—take up running and invite himself to join her.

"We didn't find any evidence at the beach to contradict your story, but nothing to support it, either," Davies added. "The crime scene team reported to me half an hour ago. There was nothing at the beach to help at all."

"Footprints?" Sawyer asked, ignoring the look Kelsey was giving him.

"Shiloh and her team found footprints, but it's nearly impossible to get a good footprint from sand. If this had happened on some of our red clay, we could have made a mold and identified the type of shoe, shoe size, and approximate height and weight of the wearer— lots of information." Davies shook his head. "But in the sand, they're more like indents than footprints. So they could tell someone had been there, but nothing more than that."

"Why did you come by, then?" Kelsey asked.

"I wanted to check on you." The chief shook his head.

"It doesn't seem fair that you come back to town to help out and now you're dealing with all this."

"Well," Kelsey's voice seemed a little *too* light, like she was trying too hard, "I didn't come back to help but to work."

"You did the right thing, Kelsey. The museum will benefit from having someone like you assess it, with your knowledge of Treasure Point and the history of our area."

She seemed to shrug off the compliment. "I'm just doing my job."

"Nevertheless, the town appreciates it. I enjoyed working with you at the police department, but I saw those books you'd read on your breaks, about antiques. It's admirable, what you did, working all those years to save—"

"Thanks, chief," she interrupted him, and darted a quick glance Sawyer's way. What was that about?

"All right, we'll be going then." The chief moved toward the door, followed by Lieutenant Davies. "I'm sorry we didn't have more to report. We're still waiting on ballistics from the bullets from the other night, as well as the autopsy on Michael Wingate. We've also been interviewing all of his friends and associates to see if they know of any conflicts or enemies he might have had. Hopefully one of those will tell us something."

"I'll look forward to hearing from you. Let me know if I can help at all," she called as they were leaving. The chief was already halfway to the car.

"You just focus on staying safe," Davies said.

Then both men climbed into the car and drove away.

Sawyer looked at Kelsey. She looked away.

"What did he mean, Kelsey, about you reading books on your breaks?"

She waved him off as she headed back toward the table and the dinner they hadn't finished. "Just books about antiques I used to read in my spare time."

"Were they for college?"

"Not then, no."

"I'd assumed—"

"You really shouldn't do that." Kelsey cut him off and reached for the bowl of biscuits, shoved them at him. "Biscuit?"

"Would you quit trying to feed me and answer my questions?"

"Are you kidding? We're south of the Mason-Dixon. Feeding men is in my DNA."

"Please, Kelsey."

"There's no reason to discuss it. It's in the past and that's... It's past. It's over. Whatever, let's move on."

"I would, but *you* don't seem to be willing to move on, at least not where you and me are concerned."

"There *really* was never a 'you and me.'"

"Why didn't you go to college after high school, Kelsey? I'll just ask you that, since it's what I'm really wondering about. You were the smartest in our class, and I always thought you'd go right after graduation, not get a job immediately."

"Not all of us were Hamiltons."

"And now there you go with that again. Really?"

"Hey, if the silver spoon fits."

Sawyer stood, pushed his chair back from the table and shook his head. "I don't know what's up with you, Kelsey. I'm trying to help you. But for reasons I don't get, my help is the only help you're dead set on not having. That's fine. I hope you have a nice night."

Sawyer let himself out, walked back to his truck.

But he didn't bother putting the key in the ignition.

She didn't want him to be part of her life, fine. That didn't mean he had to abandon her when he was pretty sure she needed someone helping her stay safe.

Kelsey had been surprised at how much she'd wanted to run after Sawyer and tell him she didn't mean it.

Except she did. Not being able to go to college right after high school was one of those life-defining moments for Kelsey. Maybe some people would consider that silly, but learning, getting that degree, had been *her* dream, not her parents' or anyone else's. And she'd worked hard in school, done everything she could to earn the scholarships she had known she would need to make her dreams happen.

And then Sawyer interfered.

One scholarship competition, the biggest one, one she'd been so sure she had in the bag that she'd let a couple of other applications sit ignored because she'd been so sure she'd win this one. It had made sense at the time—why split her efforts between ten or so scholarship applications when pouring all her focus into this one would give her the rest of the money she'd needed. One speech, one he'd decided to give at the last minute, when until then Kelsey hadn't seen much competition in the list of names on the speaking schedule. And the award she'd been counting on to send her to college had gone to someone else. Someone who *hadn't even needed it.*

Kelsey stalked over to where Sawyer had been sitting, picked up his plate and moved to the trash can. She dumped the uneaten dinner into it and banged the plate on the side of the can to get the remaining food off.

That and because it made her feel better.

How dare Sawyer push her, try to make her talk about

these things? He'd wreaked enough havoc in her life. Why couldn't he just leave her alone?

She went back to her seat and sat down, but her appetite was gone. She wrapped her leftovers and put them in the fridge, then headed up the stairs. On her way up, she noticed the marker stains on the walls that the last tenants had left. That was something else she'd need to take care of before her parents put the house on the market. Like she needed anything else to think about.

Deciding it would help relax her to focus on her work for the museum, Kelsey went immediately to the large desk in her room and surveyed the papers and photographs she'd spread out there when she was working the other night. She'd been cataloguing items from the museum, taking pictures of them, then filling out sheets estimating their value and calculating the appropriate amount of insurance she'd recommend to the historical society. She hoped to have everything ready for Jim, the head of the society, to approve as soon as possible, but everything kept getting pushed back.

Maybe she could get some work done tonight, bump that timeline up a little.

It was after one in the morning by the time she noticed how late it was. Thankfully the pile on the desk was more organized, and she'd gotten a substantial amount of work done. It would have to do for tonight. She was exhausted. She readied herself for bed in record time and checked the doors to make sure they were locked. Everything was closed up tight. She should be safe tonight. Although the thought of sleeping when someone was trying to kill her was intimidating.

When she walked past the window in her room she raised her eyebrows and blinked a few times to make sure she was seeing what she thought she was.

Sawyer Hamilton's truck, still parked in her drive-way. Still watching out for her. Was the man planning to stay there all night?

And how could he keep being so kind to her when she kept pushing him away, and not very nicely, again and again?

Kelsey had slept fitfully all night, and had thought about trudging downstairs at a little after three in the morning to apologize to Sawyer. But she knew that doing so would be foolish when his purpose in being out there was to keep her safe. Leaving the house in the darkness was probably not doing her best to protect herself—and anyway, he was probably sleeping, and it would be rude to wake him.

In the morning she dressed with a little extra care, which was ridiculous, but Kelsey already felt insecure about the way she'd treated Sawyer yesterday and some-how it made her feel better to think that she'd be look-ing her best. After that, she headed for the kitchen and made coffee, drinking it while she worked on break-fast—scrambled eggs, leftover biscuits from last night and bacon.

She set out two plates, put the food on the table, then took a deep breath and headed outside.

With the way the new day was beginning, the nearly cloudless sky, and the warmth of the Georgia summer, it didn't feel like anything could go wrong today. It was the sort of day when she wished she were the sort of per-son who didn't take work so seriously so that she could play hooky and take a beach day.

But Kelsey wouldn't do that. She shook off the idea before it could plant itself in her mind.

Instead she lifted her hand to knock lightly on Sawyer's window. He was asleep, head leaned back against the headrest, his hair looking a little more rumpled than usual, the same with his shirt.

It only took a couple of knocks for him to sit up straight, shake his head and roll down the window. "I must have nodded off just as the sun was coming up. I tried to stay awake."

Nothing in his tone gave away that he was harboring any kind of grudge from their argument the night before. Had he forgotten? Kelsey was pretty sure she hadn't exagerated how awful she'd been in her mind. He deserved an apology.

"Listen, Sawyer, I can't believe you stayed out here all night."

"It was nothing. Someone needed to, Kelsey."

The way he said her name, the particular way his masculine Southern drawl stretched it out, warmed her inside. Still, though, the longer she was out here, the more uncomfortable she got. Being out in the open like this couldn't be a good idea, could it?

"I have more to say…" She hesitated, then rushed out her words. "Can you come inside for a minute?"

"Yeah, I'd love to stretch my legs."

Kelsey didn't wait for him to say anything else, just hurried back inside. By the time she'd made it past the front door her heart was pounding in her ears, but nothing had happened. She was safe. Treasure Point had never been her favorite place. She didn't hold the same nostalgia for it that a lot of townspeople seemed to, but the place had never given her a reason to feel scared, even when she was a police officer. That had all changed now and it felt oddly like a betrayal, although Kelsey didn't know why. For one thing, the town itself didn't have thoughts or feelings to make betrayal possible, obviously. And for another, hadn't Kelsey betrayed the town first by leaving, without a single look back, as soon as she was able?

For all the good that had done her. Maybe the naysayers had been right, after all—maybe a small-town girl like her never would amount to much. Maybe coming from a small town meant she was destined for small things.

"Is that bacon?" Sawyer sniffed as he stepped inside and locked the door behind him. She appreciated his concern for her safety.

"I fixed breakfast. As a thank-you…and an apology. I was out of line last night and I'm sorry."

Sawyer met her eyes, something that Kelsey found surprisingly comforting. "It's okay. It's been a rough few days for you."

"It's still no excuse."

"Well, it's fine. No hard feelings."

"Let's eat, then. I need to get to the museum before it gets too late and I'm sure you must have places to be…" She hadn't realized until then that she didn't know exactly what Sawyer was doing in Treasure Point. "What, um…" As they sat down at the table, she searched for a way to ask the question that wouldn't come across as "Why are you here?" but had trouble finding one. She finally settled on, "What brings you back to town?"

"The museum reopening. Aunt Mary's health isn't doing the best, and while my parents are in town they have a lot of other engagements, so since someone from the family needed to be present for the ceremonies and everything, and it was a bigger commitment than my parents could handle, they asked me to do it."

"So you're literally here because you're a Hamilton."

"I thought you were sorry about—"

"No, I'm not saying it that way." Kelsey's cheeks flushed. "I just think it's amazing that you're back in town for that reason, and yet you…you're here right when I guess I needed someone."

Sawyer set his fork down. His eyes met her eyes as he lifted his coffee mug and took a long sip of coffee. "Speaking of which, I have a proposition for you."

"Okay."

"I've been thinking about whoever is after you. And I think it has to do with the museum."

"I agree."

"Really?"

"Yep." She nodded. "If I'd witnessed some random person's murder, it would be obvious the killer was after me just because I was a witness, but it isn't like that."

"No, it's not."

"I think Michael Wingate was killed because of his job, so I think I would have been in danger because of mine, since I'd be in the best position to uncover whatever it is he was killed for."

"I completely agree. Thought about it last night in my truck."

"So I want to do my job today at the museum while trying to learn what Michael could have known or seen that would have made him a target. There's one exhibit in particular I have suspicions about, but I could be wrong. In any case, I feel like if I can figure that out, maybe I can pass it on to Clay or someone else at the police department, and maybe it'll give them a lead to follow."

"You do know you don't have to do this investigation yourself."

"You said that last night," she said in a dry tone.

"But, really, you trust these guys. Let them do their jobs."

Kelsey shook her head. "Working at the museum and examining the exhibits is *my* job. I'll just be keeping an eye out for anything that might have a dangerous connection. And anyway, something about the way the chief was talking last night makes me think they don't have much yet. They need all the help they can get."

"If you're determined to do this, then here's my proposition." He looked at her for a long minute, not saying anything, and once again she was a little disconcerted by how comfortable she felt under his gaze and how much it unsettled her at the same time—but in a nice way. A butterflies-in-her-stomach sort of way, oddly enough.

"I'm ready."

SEVEN

"If it has something to do with the museum, you'll need to do more research into whatever it is to make sense of it," Sawyer began, leading into his semibrilliant—code for "potentially crazy"—plan. "If whatever set the killer off has to do with the museum, there's probably a specific reason he chose to attack and you'll need to do more research to see what could have triggered him."

"True. I agree."

"I happen to have access to part of Aunt Mary's library. Most of it was destroyed in the fire there a few years ago, but some had been stored in boxes at my parents' house—a lot of it duplicates to what my aunt had in her house already. It's all in boxes in my parents' attic right now, but still, it's probably the most complete in this area as far as historical records, especially as they relate to Treasure Point. You let me come with you to the museum while you work, help make sure you stay alive, give you an unofficial partner in your very unofficial investigation, and I'll let you use the library as a resource."

He'd won her over with the books. Sawyer could see it on her face even as she pretended to keep considering it. He managed to keep his smile from becoming a broad grin, but just barely.

Finally she verbalized what he'd already seen. "Okay, I'll do it."

"Great." He looked at his watch. "Now we need to hurry or you'll be late."

"I set my own hours, actually, so I don't have to be there at the same time every day."

"That must be nice."

She shrugged. "It has pros and cons. I appreciate the flexibility, but the nature of the job sometimes means I'm working all day long with no breaks and staying past five because that's just how it works out."

"And did you tell me you're working this job and another?"

The look on her face said something, but Sawyer wasn't sure what.

"Yes. An estate on St. Simons."

"Swanky?"

Kelsey laughed. "I'm pretty sure no one has used that word this side of the year 2000."

"Hey, I don't see any good reason to give up a perfectly functional word."

"Whatever. But yes, it's quite *swanky*. Their antiques collection is almost unfathomable for a private collector."

"I don't know how you usually do research to estimate insurance values, but my aunt has quite a few antiques books you're welcome to look through, too, if you think any of those could help you out."

"I'd love that." She took another sip of coffee. "But why are you helping me so much? I should have asked you this earlier. What's in it for you?"

"Knowing I got to help out and keep a former classmate alive isn't good enough?"

She shook her head. "You slept in your truck. That's above and beyond. What else is there?"

So much more. Not the least of which was the fact that he'd pieced together what she hadn't said last night in that explosive conversation. His suspicions last night had been correct about that scholarship—the one that had given him the chance to double major in business and marine biology. The Hamiltons might have had plenty of money, but his father had made it clear that business was what Sawyer was supposed to focus on, and that was what the money would be going toward.

The man hadn't realized his son would figure out another way to pay for the additional major, but Sawyer was nothing if not resourceful. His dad still hadn't been thrilled, not seeing the point and sure that his business studies would suffer, but Sawyer had managed to keep above a 3.0 GPA and hang on to that scholarship all four years, and had come out with one degree that kept him from alienating his family, and one that gave him the skills to do something meaningful and personally rewarding.

Would he change anything if he could go back? Sawyer couldn't honestly say, even after being confronted with the reality last night of all it had cost Kelsey, the years she'd had to wait to pursue her own dreams. But he had guilt—a nice, large helping—and doing something like this for her helped to alleviate some of it.

Besides, the only other thing he had going on in town were family obligations, which weren't his favorite. Spending time with a woman who was his match in so many ways—not romantically, but her intellect, her sense of humor. He could think of worse things to do than finally build a friendship with her, the way he'd wanted to years ago.

"It's worth it to me. Just know that."

Kelsey didn't ask any more questions out loud. But her eyes were still full of them as she cleared the table and they both loaded into Sawyer's truck and headed for the museum—he didn't like the idea of her driving when she could so easily be forced off the road in her small SUV. His truck would be better protection.

"So, where do we start?" Kelsey asked, after they pulled in. Sawyer was surprised she'd asked him, but then she continued talking. Apparently it had been a general question, not directed at him specifically. "Maybe they'll let me into the room where the murder took place…"

"What?"

She'd already climbed out of the truck by then, so Sawyer followed her, looking around for anything that could have been a threat. He didn't have any training in situational awareness, but it didn't hurt to be conscious of his surroundings.

Clay Hitchcock was posted by the front door of the museum. "Morning, Clay," Kelsey said as she approached.

"Good morning."

"There are more officers here than yesterday," Kelsey commented, a slight frown on her face. "Do you know why?"

Clay looked around, like he was trying to see if anyone was listening. "The alarm system was triggered last night."

"Really?"

He nodded. "They didn't get all the way in. We had an officer here all night, so as soon as the alarm was triggered, he went around to the back of the building and announced himself, and whoever it was got away."

"But they'll be back."

"Maybe, maybe not—now that they know we've bumped up police presence here."

"I wonder what they were after…"

"It's related to the murder, though?" Sawyer asked. "Is that what y'all think, or could it be pure coincidence?"

"It's not something I can discuss with either of you, since you're not officers." Clay smiled apologetically. "Sorry, you know how it goes, Kelsey."

She nodded, surprising Sawyer. He'd expected her to put up more of a fight to be kept in the loop, even though it wasn't really protocol. But Clay was a good guy, one with real integrity, which was probably why Kelsey didn't bother to press with any more questions. Clay wouldn't answer them, and it would just create tension for him to have to keep telling them no.

But Sawyer did smile a little as they went inside and Clay muttered under his breath. "Let me just say that I've never been one to believe in coincidences."

"So, what were they after?"

Kelsey turned to Sawyer, who'd just voiced the question that had been on her mind.

"Whatever it is, they didn't get it. Not if they left immediately after hearing there were police here."

"So how do we figure out what it is? Where do we start?"

It was somewhat odd to have confident Sawyer Hamilton asking her for direction, but Kelsey couldn't say she minded much. Actually, she appreciated the fact that he seemed to be perfectly willing to let her call the shots and be her sidekick in this…whatever she was doing.

Whether she should be doing it or not.

"Let's stick with my original plan, before we heard about the break-in. I want to go in the room where the murder took place and make sure there's nothing suspicious in there."

"You were there, though, so you'd have seen if anything was left or taken."

"True," Kelsey agreed as she started down the hallway in the direction of that room. "But I want to walk through it anyway, go through what might have happened. There are a still a lot of things that room could tell us. While the location of the murder might have been coincidental, there's a chance that something triggered it, something in that room. Know what I mean?"

"I do." She heard the respect in his voice, and it meant a lot to her. It might not have been her dream career, but she'd done her best to be a good law enforcement officer, had tried hard every day and had felt like she'd done a good job right up until the last case she'd worked.

But she didn't want to think about that right now. Right now she was doing two things she was good at, dealing with the antiques in this museum that needed to be properly insured, and investigating this case that had turned personal. Better to focus on those things, on her successes, than the negatives.

"Let me know what you see. I'm afraid my specialty is more marine animals and their habitats," Sawyer said with a laugh.

Kelsey stopped walking, and turned around. "Wait. I thought you were in business?"

He shook his head.

"But you were, right?" She didn't finish the thought, but it didn't really need finishing, it was so predictable—*but you're a Hamilton*. The Hamilton family was known for its business successes and, in the younger generations, for its pride and arrogance about them. Mary Hamilton had never been pretentious. Old South proper, and a bit like royalty, yes, but she was also down-to-earth and caring. Kelsey couldn't say the same thing about her nephew, Sawyer's dad. The man had always struck her as one of the coldest people she'd ever met, but with a great head for business, as was evidenced by the success he'd had with his investments over the years.

"I was working with my dad until recently."

"Kelsey, is that you?" Lieutenant Davies walked out of the room she'd been heading into, and nodded when he saw her. "I thought so. What are you up to this morning?"

"I'm finishing up the first pass of my assessment. I have this room and then one more," she said smoothly. It was the truth. Not all of it, but she didn't need to elaborate to anyone, especially anyone at the police department, that she was running her own unsanctioned investigation.

Davies nodded, his face looking as serious as it always did. The man had never known how to have fun and relax like the rest of the guys she'd worked with on the force. He was all work, all the time, it seemed, and Kelsey guessed that when the chief retired in the next few years, the lieutenant would be a shoo-in for the job.

"I'll let you get to it then."

"Are you and Clay both sticking around here today?" Kelsey should probably have an idea of how many officers were around so she could make sure that she wasn't doing any obvious investigating when any of them were around.

"Yes, and one of the newer guys, Officer Dixon. You

don't need to worry about your safety—we'll be keeping an eye out for any trouble."

She nodded. "Thanks."

"Have a good day." He walked down the hallway toward the main section of the museum. He wasn't being as openly hostile as he'd been when she'd returned, something for which Kelsey was thankful. Apparently he'd realized she was innocent in all this and had decided to let the past go. When he was gone, Kelsey walked into the room where everything had started.

She got chills as soon as she looked around. It was daylight, that was different, but the knowledge that a man's life had ended right here, that she'd been a witness to it, as it was happening, was weighty. The anxiety could easily be suffocating if she didn't deal with it the right way.

Another run after work today might be in order. This time she'd just have to ask Sawyer to come with her.

Kelsey took a deep breath, tried to ground herself in the present. It was daylight, she repeated in her mind again, needing to cement that thought for herself. No one was here killing anyone right now. And if she turned around and left this room now, then she couldn't finish her job and get out of this town, and she also would be walking away from potential clues to who was after her.

"So…" Sawyer's voice was low, but it still startled her. She shot him a look and he smiled a little—smiled in the face of one of her best glares, which was slightly insulting—and shook his head. "How did you get started with this job?"

"Oh, it was something I've always wanted to do. I love antiques and it seemed like a good career move."

"Didn't you enjoy being an officer, though?"

Kelsey could do without that conversation today. "Sure. I need to focus now, if you don't mind. Sorry."

Sawyer took her hint and Kelsey got to work.

Kelsey steered clear of the far wall where the double doors that opened onto the balcony were. She didn't need to get *that* close to the scene of the crime today. Instead she focused on the built-in bookshelves on either side of the door where they'd come in, and on the displays on the other two walls. The books were relatively standard fare for old books. From the index she'd been given, she knew that none were rare copies or first editions. Most of their value, in her opinion, was sentimental. There were histories of the Hamiltons and some of the other families who had lived in Treasure Point since its founding. There were several books of maps, some histories of coastal Georgia. All of it was lovely and added character to the museum and another layer of authenticity, but none of it required much thinking on her part in terms of the valuation of the items.

The first exhibit in the room was about Blackbeard, the famous pirate who'd spent time around the Treasure Point coast. In fact, as the display reminded her, he was rumored to have had a relationship with one of the ancestors of the Hamiltons. The display also included a small amount of pirate treasure—a few gold coins— and a note about Officer Shiloh Cole being responsible for its recovery—she'd have to ask her about that sometime—as well as an old book that had been signed by Blackbeard and a few other small things.

The other exhibit was similar, but dealt with a wider variety of pirates, some of whose names Kelsey recognized and some she didn't. This exhibit drew her in, just as it would a visitor to the museum, because it was about undiscovered shipwrecks that were rumored to lie off the Georgia coast.

There was a map in the exhibit with shaded areas where experts hypothesized the wrecks might be found, mostly in more protected areas of the ocean in and among the barrier islands. A framed note beside the map indicated that the Treasure Point Historical Society hoped to eventually contract trained divers to search for and perhaps recover some of the articles from the ships for use in the museum. It would take more time and federal permission, so Kelsey wished them well with that. Shipwrecks with such historical significance would be fought over by far bigger contenders than Treasure Point, but she admired their hopefulness and had to admit that it gave the exhibit a nice touch, an extra hint of excitement.

The exhibit did have one artifact, the plaque beside its case identified it as a chart divider, and explained that it had been recovered on the beach near Treasure Point and was thought to have washed up from one of the wrecks off the coast.

"Isn't that interesting?" Sawyer said from behind her. Kelsey jumped. She'd almost forgotten he was behind her, she'd been so enthralled by her work.

This, *this* was why she'd chosen this job, because it was so much more a passion than it could ever be a paycheck. She cared about what she was doing.

"Which part of it?" Kelsey asked, even though her answer would be "yes" for just about any of it.

"How it says that items like this were often the most common sort of pirate treasure. I think of coins, you know?"

Kelsey nodded. "You saw the one across the room, right?"

"I did."

Kelsey looked back at the sign Sawyer had motioned to. Apparently navigational tools were a common "treasure" that pirates had been able to sell for profit—but something they could also carry around easily and use until they found a buyer. That hadn't been covered in any of her history classes that she could remember.

She made a few notes in her iPad, then looked toward the French doors that led to the balcony.

"Are you going out there?" he asked.

Kelsey wanted to say no. But if she was really going to investigate this, she couldn't ignore the scene of the crime. She exhaled. "Yes."

She took a few tentative steps in that direction, then looked back at Sawyer, who hadn't moved. "Are you coming?" She was surprised at how much she wanted him to.

"If that's what you want." He walked toward her, even offered his hand. She took it—for moral support of course, nothing else—and opened the door with her other hand.

It looked…like a balcony. Nothing about the scene up here suggested someone had been pushed off. She leaned forward a little until she could see the stains on the ground beneath told the truth about what had happened here.

But there was no new evidence, which meant she could leave the balcony and not come back. She hurried inside, dropping Sawyer's hand as soon as she'd shut the door behind them.

Then she turned to Sawyer. "I've got to head to St. Simons now. You could drop me off at my house so I can get my car, or—"

"Let me come."

After the way he'd made sacrifices to keep her safe

last night by sleeping in his truck, she didn't have the heart to refuse him. Besides, even with a gun secured at her waistline, there was really no substitute for the way Sawyer's broad shoulders and overall strength made her feel.

Safe. They made her feel safe.

As she thought about them, her eyes went to his arms, which filled out the sleeves of his polo like he'd spent more time outside than in an office in the last few years.

Kelsey jerked her eyes away as soon as she realized she was noticing Sawyer in a way that had very little to do with tolerating an unofficial bodyguard. Seeing him like that, as a man rather than just someone who wanted to help, or a former classmate…it couldn't work. She wasn't opposed to the idea of a relationship with some-one, although it had taken her years to make the strides she'd finally made in her career, and it would take a special man to be able to handle that. But job passions aside, Sawyer could never be the man for her. The whole Atlantic Ocean's worth of water was under that bridge, whether he was aware of the reasons or not, and try as she might—because she *had* tried—Kelsey had never been able to forgive his youthful pride in going out for that speech contest that had ended up costing her the scholarship she'd needed so desperately.

"Yes, you can come," she said to him with a little more distance in her voice than she'd had before, then she turned out of the room she couldn't wait to escape and headed down the hallway.

EIGHT

Every time Sawyer started to feel like he was getting to know twenty-eight-year-old Kelsey, something happened to transport him back to eighteen again and remind him of why she wouldn't let them be friends. Judging by Kelsey's attitude at times, being casual acquaintances was more than enough for them to try to handle. Even though he understood that she was upset about the scholarship, there had to be more to it than that. What kept getting between them?

He followed her to the front door, then stepped out first, something she shot him a look for, but even though there was a substantial police presence at the museum, he felt better knowing he'd seen the outside, scanned it for threats, before she had. No, he didn't have law enforcement training like she did, but he was observant and could pay attention to details, especially when it involved a possible threat. He'd also been raised in the South. While he believed women to be fully capable—and he believed Kelsey to be *more* than fully capable of taking care of herself—he also believed that a good man was willing to take on some danger so a woman didn't *have* to.

Along those lines, he walked to Kelsey's side of the truck and opened the door for her.

When he closed the door behind her and circled the front of the truck, he realized that this felt oddly like a date. Kelsey Jackson was the kind of woman he wouldn't mind taking out, getting to know. His chances of getting her to agree to that were pretty slim, though.

As he climbed into the truck, he glanced over at her, and smiled a little at the way the sunlight coming through her dark red hair almost made it look like it was on fire. Didn't that just suit her personality well?

"All right, Kelsey. I've had about enough of the weird one-step-forward as friends and two-steps-back stuff. This isn't the first time it's happened, so would you mind telling me what's up?" Sawyer wasn't one to beat around the bush, but maybe Kelsey didn't know that, because she looked surprised at his pointed question.

"I want to ask you what you mean and fake ignorance, but it won't work for me, will it?" she asked without looking at him. He admired both her honesty and her perceptiveness.

"No."

"I need to let it go, Sawyer. It's stupid and it's petty and it's embarrassing."

"How?"

"You know where we're going right?"

"St. Simons."

"To the Medlin Estate. It's on the north side. Just take the normal highway and roads to the island and I'll give you more directions when we get there."

"Sounds great, but you aren't getting out of this conversation."

"Fine. It's about that speech contest. The one for the scholarship."

So it *was* about that. But was that really all there was to it?

"What about it?"

She took a deep breath. "You don't get it, do you?"

"What?"

"You asked me why I became a police officer. It's because I have always wanted to do the job I'm doing now, to work with antiques and have a job that provided a more secure life, with less guesswork, more certainty. But doing that meant going to college, which my parents couldn't afford. I worked summers and after school, saved every penny I could, but when you got that scholarship, that was the rest of the money I was counting on. So instead of starting this process at eighteen, I had to wait until I was in my early twenties and had earned enough money working a job that wasn't a career for me to do it."

It was everything he'd wondered, confirmed. Except possibly worse.

"I did need the scholarship, Kelsey."

"You... What?"

"Look, it's a long story and I don't want to get into family drama. But I wanted to major in marine biology and that wasn't an option without the scholarship. Can we leave it at that?"

"I thought you majored in business. Didn't you tell me that earlier?"

"Double majored."

"Oh."

She seemed to be digesting that. At least, Sawyer guessed so, because she didn't say anything else, which was fine with him.

"How much farther to the estate?" he finally asked when he couldn't stand the quiet anymore.

"Not far."

After a few more minutes of silence, Kelsey spoke again. "Look, I'm going to be honest with you, Sawyer. I don't know what this confession of yours changes. Maybe nothing."

"You're going to keep holding on to a decade-old grudge? Even now that you understand it wasn't about beating you?"

Sawyer knew he was being extremely blunt, but Kelsey could handle it. They were adults now, and whether he was her favorite person or not, it didn't seem unreasonable to think they could get along relatively well in small doses.

"You're right." Kelsey exhaled the admission just as they were pulling through the gates of an estate that Sawyer guessed was the Medlin Estate. She met his eyes. "I'll work on letting it go."

"Thank you. Now, how do you want to do this? Do you want me to just follow you around? Is anyone going to wonder why you have a plus-one with you at work?"

"I don't think so. The Medlins are in Europe right now, so it's only the staff and they tend to not ask questions."

They had a whole contingent of staff, even when they weren't in town? That sounded kind of over the top.

He parked the truck and they walked around to the back of the house, where Kelsey knocked on a door. Only moments passed before a woman in a maid's uniform answered the door. She showed them inside and then, as Kelsey had said, left them to their own devices. Sawyer couldn't resist an impressed whistle as he looked around at the opulence of the house.

"These people are seriously wealthy."

"You're one to comment on something like that."

"What? I'm just saying that judging by the house, they don't seem like the warmest of people. And like they appreciate money. Am I wrong?"

"The Medlins have never been anything but nice to me."

"And I suppose you're implying that the same can't be said for the Hamiltons?" Sawyer knew he had pushed it enough today with the way he'd pressed her about the scholarship earlier, so if she didn't answer him, he wouldn't pursue the topic.

Kelsey said nothing. Sawyer still wondered, though. He couldn't let go of the idea that there was more to her grudge against him than she'd admitted. He was relatively sure he'd never done anything to seem above her in any way. His parents? It wouldn't surprise him, but that was a can of worms he wasn't willing to open right now.

It did serve to remind him, though, that even if he was finding himself fascinated with her—her intelligence, her determination, the contradictions that made up who Kelsey Jackson was—it was pointless. They could never be more than friends. There were just too many things between them.

They moved from a well-decorated, museum-like living room into a well-decorated, museum-like kitchen. Antiques in the kitchen? Sawyer wouldn't have believed it, but sure enough, several things that looked old and expensive sat on the counters as decorations. Kelsey would have known what they were. All Sawyer knew was that it was ridiculous.

"I don't get why anyone would want to live like this."

She turned to him with a sharp frown. "Why?"

"It's not homey. It's just a collection." He'd had

enough of those growing up in his parents' house—
and theirs wasn't nearly this over the top.

Kelsey shrugged. "It doesn't have to be your thing."

"Good. It's not."

Sawyer's phone rang, saving him from the rest of
that conversation. He was glad to get away from it. He
was getting a little tired of the way Kelsey kept shoving
their differences in his face, as if she wanted to prove
to him that they were totally incompatible.

Fine. He got the message.

Kelsey had spent more time than she'd planned to
at the Medlin Estate. The antiques there were beautiful, and she was thankful she got to be the one to look
at them and do this job, and simultaneously anxious to
prove herself, despite her limited experience.

Because of that, she'd taken extra time and care there,
which had made it take up more of the day than she'd intended. She was falling behind everywhere. Frustrating,
but something that happened. Even so, she hadn't been
able to walk away from the Medlin Estate until close to
dinner time. There had just been too much to do.

Sawyer had dropped her off at home without saying
much—she couldn't blame him, she hadn't been very
good company. She'd gone inside, showered, and sat
down with her iPad and notes about the museum only
to realize she'd started on one of the rooms but never
finished. She glanced at her watch. Not too late. She
climbed back into her car, drove through a barbeque
stand for dinner, and then kept driving back into town
and straight to the Treasure Point History Museum.

There was a lone squad car parked at the corner of the
parking lot, and even though it should have made Kelsey
feel better, the reminder of the crime made her shiver,

goose bumps chased each other up her arms. She was thankful they were here so she wasn't completely alone. She waved at the officer, a young recruit she didn't know by name, and then headed inside.

She needed to spend more time in the room next door to the one where the murder had taken place, although it gave her the shivers to think of being so close to the scene of the crime again. Even though the presence of the police officer should mean she was safe, part of her wanted to call Sawyer. But then she remembered how she'd monopolized his time all day and not been very nice to him, either. The truth was, she was embarrassed by how she'd acted toward him, but she didn't know how to fix it.

Kelsey needed to hurry up and do her job here so she could get out of this town, and more importantly, out of Sawyer Hamilton's life. Who would have guessed that they'd clash worse now in their late twenties than they had in high school? Although, to be fair, it was Kelsey doing the clashing, both then and now—something else she didn't want to admit. Sawyer, especially in the past few days, had been a perfect gentleman.

Thoughts of his easygoing smile came way too easily to her mind. No, no, no. She would not think of that smile. She'd been one of the few girls in high school who hadn't been charmed by it, but she'd had enough life experience to know how much a charming man could make a woman forget.

Pushing her thoughts away from Sawyer, she focused on the task ahead of her—assessing the contents of the last room in the museum. What would happen to the museum, with the murder of the curator hanging over it? She wanted to believe the killer would be found and the case wrapped up quickly, for the museum's sake as well as for her own, but Kelsey was also realistic. A case of this depth could take months to solve. Kelsey didn't have months to spend in Treasure Point.

She had a gorgeous apartment in downtown Savannah with rent too high for it to sit empty. She had to finish these two assignments to the satisfaction of her clients and bosses, and come back victorious.

That was easier said than done at this point. Kelsey wasn't struggling with the antiques insurance at all—that part of her job was coming naturally to her, even if it had been slowed down a bit because of the murder. It was the fact that Treasure Point seemed desperate to get its hooks back in her, to have her stay, even if it was against her will.

Kelsey sat down at the desk in the corner of this room. It wouldn't stay here when the museum was officially opened, but for now it was an extra place that Kelsey and the museum board members could do their work without leaving the museum. She set her bag down, settled in with her iPad and the photos she'd taken on it earlier, and began looking through them.

Kelsey worked for another hour, both at the desk and moving around the room documenting and assessing its contents. She'd just stopped in front of a case containing old letters written by Treasure Point residents—interesting, but not highly valuable—when she heard a noise. It had to be the building settling, right? She listened for a minute but didn't hear anything else. Still, the place was empty and lonely...

She pulled her phone out and called Sawyer.

"Hello?"

She felt the tension drain from her shoulders and told herself it had nothing to do with Sawyer himself, and more to do with the fact that she was just eager for a connection to some human being, *any* human being.

"Hey, it's Kelsey."

"Where are you?"

"I'm in the museum."

"It's late. Why?"

"I realized I hadn't finished all I meant to today."

"But you'd already put in a full day. Surely they let you have some downtime, even in your job, right?"

"I can't afford to fall further behind here. I need to finish."

"So you can get out of this hick town and back to somewhere that matters, right?"

"I know that Sawyer Hamilton isn't looking down on me for wanting to get back to my job, back to my life in the city. It's not like you live here anymore, either. You left to chase success the same as I did."

"Actually, according to my father, I've been running from success," he mumbled.

"What was that?" Kelsey had heard him fine, but she didn't understand the words.

"Never mind." She could almost see him shaking his head, the longer part of his hair over his forehead moving slightly as he did so. It was shorter than it had been in high school, not that classic preppy style that had been so popular among boys in the South when she was younger. This was an updated version, something that reminded her of the boy he'd been, but that left no doubt that he'd grown up since then.

Something that was really getting in the way of her plan to keep trying to dislike him.

"Anyway, I guess I should let you go," Kelsey finally said. She hadn't heard anything else and suddenly felt silly for having called him.

"What did you call for?"

"Nothing, it's fine."

"What, Kelsey?"

"Seriously. Nothing."

His hesitation said he wasn't buying it, but he was too much a gentleman to push the issue anymore. "All right. Let me know if you need anything."

Something in the kindness of his tone broke down some of her stubbornness and her shoulders relaxed. "Sawyer?" she said, taking a deep breath.

"Yeah?"

"About earlier. I was kind of a jerk with the way I talked to you, and I'm sorry." And she was. Kelsey waited for his response.

"It's okay. Don't worry about it anymore," he said in a voice that sounded like he meant it. He was incredibly quick to forgive, Kelsey noticed, a trait she couldn't always claim in herself.

That was something else getting in the way of trying to hang on to her negative feelings toward him. And not just getting in the way of her feelings either, but changing them...

Could they be friends after all?

"Okay, well, thanks," she finished awkwardly. "And goodbye for real this time."

"Are you staying much longer?"

"Not too much." Kelsey should be done in this room within half an hour. There was always more work that *could* be done, but most of it could be done from home. She'd feel a bit safer there, behind a locked door.

"If you are, I'd like to come meet you there."

"You've done enough to help me lately. There's no need for it."

"I'm just really not sure you should be there alone, Kelsey."

And just like that, her shoulders were tensed again. She felt her eyebrows pressing together. "Why?"

"Because someone was killed there a few days ago, by the same person who has already attacked you twice."

"I'm not here alone, there's a policeman outside."

"There were a whole handful of off-duty officers the night of the gala, and some on duty, I believe. Is Michael Wingate still dead?"

Kelsey didn't want him to be right, but he was.

"Okay, you're probably right. I wasn't taking the danger seriously enough, but I had some things I really wanted to get done." She swept her gaze over the exhibit she'd been working on, one that told the story of how the first large group of Europeans had come to Treasure Point, not long after Oglethorpe had founded Savannah in 1733. Someone had managed to gather several artifacts from that time, including some dishware that was relatively valuable, as well as some personal items like hairbrushes and clothing that provided a picture of what life had been like back then.

"So, you'll leave now?" His voice wasn't one to argue with. It wasn't controlling, nothing like that, but it was clear how he felt about her being there, and for once, Kelsey didn't think she was going to argue.

"Yes, let me just double-check—"

A muffled thud on the wall next to her made her jump so much that she dropped the phone, listened to it clatter on the desk, making a much louder sound than she would have liked.

Aside from the officer who was posted outside, she was the only one here, wasn't she? She paused, half hoping maybe she'd imagined what she heard.

Another thump. Not her imagination. Had the officer outside heard it? Officer Ryan was incredibly young, but according to her cousin, was indeed old enough to be an officer. She'd texted and asked Clay after she'd met the guy the first time. Though he seemed like a nice guy, she didn't have extremely high confidence that he could hold his own against someone clever enough to have so far gotten away with murder. Kelsey only hoped he was okay.

"Kelsey?"

Sawyer was talking loudly enough that she could hear him even with the phone still lying on the desk. She reached for it quickly, turned the volume down, and pulled the phone back up to her face.

"I heard something," she whispered. "And also, talk softer."

"Okay, what did you hear?"

"I'm not sure. I mean, I don't know what caused it. It was a thump of some kind. Something relatively quiet."

"I'm coming over there."

"Don't you think that's overreacting just a bit—"

The lights went out, the gentle hum of electricity replaced by a heavy silence. She'd seen the blueprints for the building—the room with the breaker box was close. It explained the thud she'd heard. And also told her she didn't have much time until whoever was in there found her if he was looking.

And then footsteps. She wasn't alone.

"Someone is here," she whispered, then punched the volume on her phone as far down as possible so she couldn't hear anything Sawyer said—not that she wanted to ignore him, but she needed to be sure that whoever was in here with her couldn't hear anything. Kelsey slipped the phone into her pocket and slowly slid out of her chair, down onto the floor. She reached for her hip where she kept her gun, patted there and found... nothing. She'd taken it off when she'd gotten home from St. Simons, not intending to leave the house again. Then in her hurry to finish this job, she'd forgotten to put it back on before she left the house. A mistake that could cost Kelsey her life.

Hide under the desk, or try to crawl for cover somewhere? There was a closet in the corner of this room, mostly used for records, and Kelsey thought that if she could get into that—*if* there was space, which she wasn't sure about—she might be able to hide until whoever was in here was gone. Confronting him, while tempting, would just be too risky without any kind of backup. Especially since she didn't have her sidearm.

She heard another thud.

Please, God. Help. She found herself praying with a level of desperation she hadn't felt in a while. How often was it that she felt she really *needed* God? Not that He was some sort of convenient addition to her life, but like her life and breath and everything depended on Him?

Not often enough, but she couldn't think about that now as she crawled toward the closet. No, most of the time, Kelsey depended on herself. And only herself.

Tension built in her shoulders, and she squeezed her eyes shut as she took a deep, steadying breath. Her hands were starting to shake and she needed them to quit, needed every part of her to be calm right now. Strong. Brave.

Help.

This prayer was shorter than the other, but the steadiness she felt immediately afterward impacted her. Had He listened and answered that quickly?

She was feet from the door when she heard more footsteps, coming closer.

Kelsey stood, opened the closet door gently, stepped inside and shut it as quietly as she could.

The closet was pitch-black. She couldn't see the shape of the room, the outlines of the filing cabinets and lawyer's boxes she knew it held, but it didn't matter right now. It was better this way—if whoever was inside the museum was after her and trying to find her, the total darkness would work to her advantage.

Unless he went and turned the lights back on. Then she'd be as good as dead. A sitting duck with no way out.

What she wouldn't give to have a secret passageway in case she needed to make a quick escape. The old Hamilton house that the museum was modeled on had had many of them, but this new building didn't.

Instead, Kelsey fumbled as quietly as she could through the closet toward the back, using both her hands and her feet to feel for obstacles and try to gently angle herself around them. When she was as far back as she could go, she bent down again, crouched on the floor.

Nothing to do now but listen. And wait. And hope that help came. Kelsey wanted to pull out her phone for some reassurance, hoping that Sawyer had sent a text or something telling her what he planned to do. How was it that after just a few days of having him with her most of the time she'd grown so used to having him by her side whenever danger struck? She wasn't sure how she felt about it. She'd always worked alone, and even during her time at the police department when so many officers had had partners, Kelsey had always been happy to work alone. Even the few times she'd been paired up with someone, she'd been more of a lone wolf, which was why the chief had never tried to give her a permanent partner.

Seconds passed and turned into minutes. It was hard to tell how long it had been since she talked to Sawyer. Five minutes? Fifteen? Kelsey could make out small sounds now and then, but nothing that sounded threatening. Of course, she knew better than anyone that noise didn't indicate danger. The murder itself had been eerily silent.

Then the footsteps grew louder.

And the door to the closet creaked open.

NINE

Sawyer slammed on the brakes in his pickup truck and threw the door open just as three squad cars arrived at the scene.

"You need to stay in the car!" someone shouted in his direction.

He didn't even bother considering it. He'd been the one to hear Kelsey's voice. He understood more than they did what she might be going through right now, and no, he wasn't going to sit in the comfy cab of his truck and listen to music while she was in there, possibly fighting for her life.

One officer went directly to the cruiser that had already been parked in the corner by the officer stationed at the museum. Sawyer winced, hoping whoever was in it was unharmed.

"It's Officer Ryan," Officer Dalton yelled. "Unconscious, but seems okay. I think he was hit over the head."

"Stay with him, Dalton!" Hitchcock yelled.

Sawyer hurried inside the museum after the others, careful not to get in the way. Matt O'Dell shot him a little glare, but didn't try to throw him out. He'd thought the other man might understand what it was like, not being far from a newlywed.

Not that his relationship with Kelsey was anything like that. He thought she was beautiful, strong and smart. Everything that he would have valued in a relationship...

But she wasn't open to that with him, and that had to be fine with Sawyer. He'd spent years in a family that hadn't seemed to have much time for him—except for Aunt Mary. His parents had paid very little attention to him...and to each other. Their marriage had been mostly based around a business merger, and he'd never seen any signs that they truly loved or valued each other. He'd promised himself that he wouldn't repeat their mistakes. If Sawyer married, it wouldn't be for business reasons, for what society deemed a "good match" or for anything short of love.

Kelsey Jackson was a friend, someone he hoped would be a good friend one day. But she'd never love him, not like that. Even though they'd talked in the car and she'd mostly forgiven him for his part in getting the scholarship, she either still held it against him or had something else making her keep her distance from him.

But whatever she was to him now, or would be in the future, Sawyer wanted her to stay alive.

He stayed behind the officers as they cleared the house and made their way into several of the rooms.

"In here!" someone shouted. This time Sawyer followed them into the room.

Matt O'Dell went for the closet, weapon still out and ready. "She might be hiding in there," Sawyer said. "She knew something was wrong when she was on the phone with me and she's too smart to confront an intruder by herself."

The other man nodded.

The lights flickered back on. Apparently it was just the breaker and Hitchcock was able to fix it.

"I've got something here," Matt called.

From where he stood, removed from the action, he heard small scuffling noises inside the closet.

"Treasure Point PD," O'Dell said. "Are you in there, Kelsey?"

"I'm here." Her voice sounded small, but not scared. She was made of tougher stuff than that. Sawyer watched as several of the officers shifted boxes out of the way, then moved backward so that Kelsey could make her way out.

She thanked the officers who had helped her. Then she looked around the room. Scanning for threats? Or looking for him?

"Sawyer!" As soon as she spotted him, she hurried in his direction. The smile on her face made his stomach do a little flip—relief at seeing her alive, no doubt. No need for it to be more than that.

"I came as soon as I got your call," he said. "I phoned it in to 9-1-1 during the drive." He forced himself to be still, to respect the distance she kept putting between them, ignoring his own urge to pull her into a hug and feel that she was safe and uninjured.

She threw her arms around him, squeezed, then, in a split second, it seemed like she fully realized what she was doing and she let go and stepped back. "Um…thank you. I mean, for calling the police and coming here." Her cheeks were pink, but whether from the excitement of the entire situation or from embarrassment at hugging Sawyer so enthusiastically he wasn't sure.

"Of course. No problem."

"Can you tell us in your own words what happened, Kelsey?" O'Dell asked.

"Sure. I was here working late—"

"What were you working on?"

"I was just doing my job, assessing some of the artifacts and antiques from the exhibits, as the Treasure Point Historical Society asked me to."

"You're an appraiser?" O'Dell asked.

"Yes, for the Harlowe Company, an insurance group in Savannah." Kelsey was glad it was true, that she hadn't been in danger because of her determination to poke around and see if she could learn anything that would lead her to the man who was trying to kill her.

"Did you see anyone?"

She shook her head. "No. I heard a thud through the wall from the next room over."

"Could you identify what caused the thud?"

Kelsey frowned, concentrating, then shook her head. "No, I can't be sure. But there was more than one thud. After that, the lights went out and I heard footsteps in the hall. Then he came in here. The closet door opened, but I think the noise of your arrival must have scared whoever it was off."

"That's not surprising. Whoever this is has gone to great pains to keep his identity a secret. He wouldn't risk being caught, not even to kill you. And it's probable he didn't know for sure where you were inside the museum. He couldn't have been certain he'd find you in the closet, even if he was looking for you."

Kelsey nodded. "Right, that makes sense." She rubbed her arms, where goose bumps had risen during her time in the closet. It was disturbing how much of a physical effect fear could have on the body.

"Well—" O'Dell surveyed the room and then looked back at Kelsey "—you're free to go. I don't see any reason to keep you here any longer."

"I'm more than ready to go, so I appreciate that." Kelsey tried to say it in a lighthearted way, but no one even cracked a smile. She didn't blame them—none of this was funny.

"I'll follow you home," Sawyer offered.

Kelsey nodded, grabbed her bag and walked out of the room. Sawyer followed her.

She climbed into her blue Jeep and Sawyer got into his own truck. They drove the long road off the museum property without incident, and then headed toward Kelsey's house. As they drove away from the museum, there were more questions in Sawyer's mind than ever.

He followed her to her house, staying right behind her, and climbed out of his truck once he'd parked, moving fast enough that he was on the front porch of the house only a second behind her. He was barely in time to catch the door before she closed it behind her.

"Would you wait for me? It's a little hard to help keep you safe if you don't."

She raised her eyebrows. "I didn't know you were planning to get out of your truck. I thought you were just going along with me, keeping an eye on things during the drive. I don't recall keeping me safe being part of your job description."

"Well, it is. Stop being difficult."

Her head whipped up and her face was ready with a glare, but Sawyer grinned. "I was teasing about that last part."

"Okay, fine, you got me. But it's been a rough day."

"I know, Kelsey. So are you going to let me in, or just leave me standing on the porch?"

"Let you in?"

"Into your house. I don't really think you should be alone yet."

She didn't say anything, but that meant she hadn't said no yet. Maybe Sawyer was making progress showing her that he could be a good friend.

"I just don't think it's necessary."

"I could always just sit out here, I guess. It's not that uncomfortable, although I hear you have spiders on this porch."

Kelsey rolled her eyes. "Fine, come in." She stepped inside and he followed, double-checking to make sure she locked the door behind them.

He understood that she was still making her mind up about them being friends, but Sawyer wondered how long this would continue before Kelsey realized that she was in over her head with this investigation, and needed help. Not only would they have to trust each other to make sense of the things that kept happening, but there was a good chance they'd have to find a current law enforcement officer who trusted them, too, and was willing to keep them in the loop.

It was a lot to ask for someone like Kelsey, who was used to relying only on herself. Sawyer found himself whispering a small prayer as he followed her farther into the house, praying that she'd be able to trust the right people and would be willing to depend on them.

Because their ability to solve the case might depend on *that*.

Sawyer wouldn't be talked out of leaving her house unless she called someone else to stay with her or relocated somewhere else where she wouldn't be by herself, or at least wouldn't be so isolated. Kelsey wanted to fight that just as a matter of principle, the same way she fought any suggestion that she might not be able to take care of herself. She had to admit, though, she was starting to see how nice it was to have people caring about her, people who weren't depending on her for anything, but who wanted to *help* her. Still, part of her still clung to that independence. It was comfortable. It was who she was.

Is it unreasonable to want to stay in my own house, God? I don't mind taking some precautions to be safe, but should I really have to let this killer turn my life and my plans upside down?

"So, do you want some coffee?" Kelsey asked him after he'd been sitting on the couch for a minute. Much too long in Southern-hospitality time for her not to have given him at least some sort of drink option.

"I'd love some."

"Great." Honestly, she was relieved he wanted coffee. It gave her something to do with her hands, maybe a way to work some of the nervous energy out so he wouldn't notice that they were still shaking after the last incident. It also gave her space from him, something Kelsey was beginning to find that she needed. How had she spent all of high school being mean to him? He was so easy to be friends with, and would be so easy to care about more than that...

No. It didn't matter how much he helped her, how much she liked being taken care of by him, even if she didn't *need* it. A relationship would never work between them. Their lives were too different. Kelsey was ready to launch herself firmly into the business world as an antiques insurance estimator, and was looking forward to the heavy travel that came with the job. Her focus was on her career, and the opportunities it held. It wasn't going to take her around the world. Not quite yet. But it was another step in the right direction, as the company she'd joined got calls from all over the Southeast. She just needed to prove herself, and then she could start climbing the ladder.

If she didn't stop caring about him so much, if she let her heart get involved, she wouldn't be focused. Either she'd be caught up in a new relationship or she'd be heartbroken over its inevitable end. Her only option right now was being alone.

"Anything I can do?"

She jumped at Sawyer's voice. She felt she did a pretty good job with situational awareness, but Sawyer seemed to have a knack for surprising her. The man must have extraordinarily quiet shoes.

"No, I think I'm okay," she said, knowing it was true in relation to the coffee making, if not much else.

"Rattled from today at all?"

Yes—and yet she was more rattled by him than by the near encounter with the killer. Ridiculous. She dumped in two extra heaping scoops of coffee. That should knock some sense into her.

"Uh, you sure you've got the coffee under control there? It's looking a little strong."

"You're not scared of a little strong coffee, are you?"

"I can take it, but then again, I'm planning to stay up all night. Are you?"

He had a point there. But Kelsey didn't like to back down, so she dumped another scoop in. Then pressed the start button on the machine.

Sawyer raised his eyebrows and shook his head. "So, what now?"

"Well, now it takes about five minutes to go through the brewing system…"

"You know I'm not talking about the coffee."

Okay, yes, she did.

"What are you talking about, then?"

"The museum seems to be the obvious key to this murder. The curator was killed, and you mentioned the murder could have been in that room for a reason. We need to figure out if it was."

"Good idea. How did you get so good at this with no investigative experience?"

He shrugged. "It's not much different than marine biology. You see a problem or something out of the ordinary, you start to investigate it, make lists in your mind and follow up on leads and theories until you get somewhere."

So true. And Kelsey had enjoyed that in police work for a time, and thought she could do a good job at it again now, but what she really wanted was the kind of life the antiques insurance business offered—more artistic estimation based on facts and less stabs in the dark. It was exciting to chase hypotheses for a little while, but she appreciated facts. Black and white. Listening to gut instincts, chasing suspicions…she couldn't handle that anymore. There were too many opportunities to read things wrong—the way she had in that awful case with the Hamiltons.

"I guess I can see that," she replied. "I suppose if you're not planning to leave anytime soon anyway, you can help me go through my information about the contents of the room where the murder took place. I don't see anything there that could have provoked the killing, but maybe another set of eyes examining it would be good. I'm guessing you were paying less attention to the room's contents the other day and more to whether anyone was around."

He smiled. "Guilty."

Even if it had feel a little like overstepping the bounds of their relationship for him to be so protective, Kelsey had to admit that knowing he was there to watch her back the other day had allowed her to focus a little more on the work she was doing, instead of splitting her attention so she could watch what was going on around her, too.

She walked to where she'd put the leather satchel-style handbag she used as a briefcase. It was one of the possessions she was most proud of—she'd bought it with her first paycheck from the Harlowe Company, a sort of visual reminder to herself that she'd finally succeeded.

Kelsey opened the bag and rifled through the pictures she'd taken earlier that day. She'd taken them on her iPad, emailed them to herself and then printed them at the museum earlier. She pulled them out, walked to the dining room table and laid them all out, side by side. They weren't as nice looking as they could have been—she'd print them on glossy photo paper later, but she'd wanted to have hard copies at the museum so she'd settled for using the color printer and regular paper there.

Sawyer frowned. "Did you not get to the last exhibit?"

"Which one?" Kelsey scanned the pictures. She'd documented everything carefully before going to investigate the room where she'd gotten trapped.

"The one with the map of the areas where people believe there are sunken ships."

"No, I photographed that one. It was just one picture, the map, since that's all the exhibit contains."

Kelsey flipped through the pictures again. Looked up as she felt a wave of overwhelming dizziness at what she'd just realized. "It's not here." She'd left her briefcase by the desk. Someone had known she was there, no question about it. And while they might not have had time to kill her on the spot, they'd clearly had time to go through her bag and take something out. Had it been that important to the killer that she not have a picture of that map? It seemed like it, but why? And what if they'd left something, too, something dangerous?

Kelsey dropped the bag and stepped away from it, mind racing, wondering if her would-be killer had the kind of access to dangerous chemicals that could mean there could be some sort of toxin on the bag, or if that was taking her imagination too far. "Call the police," she said to Sawyer.

"On it."

As he punched the numbers on his phone, Kelsey struggled to breathe, worked to quiet her mind, but it was racing in circles like some kind of out-of-control race car. Had the killer even noticed her bag? She was assuming so, because that was the worst-case scenario in this situation, but it wasn't necessarily true. There could be another explanation for the missing photo.

Kelsey scanned the pictures again, from a distance. Everything else she'd appraised was there, it was only the picture of the map that had the general shipwreck areas that was gone. It wasn't even a picture she'd needed to take, since there was practically zero value for insurance purposes in the modern map. She'd snapped it because she was curious, because it had piqued her interest.

Apparently for good reason.

"Sawyer, you're right about the case, then," she said as pieces started to fall together in her mind. "It's something in that room. It has to do with that map, the pirate shipwreck map."

"You think that map will lead us closer to him?"

"A different sort of treasure map…" she mused. "But yes." She shivered. "This keeps getting more complicated. The other night I actually thought the murder might just be its own incident. A crime where someone lost his temper and made a mistake, you know? But the way this keeps escalating says it is more than that."

"Can you call the police station for me?"

He looked at her with a funny expression. "The police will be here any minute. I called a minute ago, the first time you asked."

She shook her head, frustrated that she wasn't able to get her thoughts out fast enough. They were darting around her brain right now, too fast for even her to keep track of, but they were good thoughts. She was starting to make sense of some things. "I know, but I have something else that can't wait. I know they cleared the rooms at the museum when you rescued me earlier to make sure the killer wasn't still lurking, but I wonder how close attention they paid to the contents of the rooms."

"You think something was stolen."

Kelsey nodded. "This map. I'm almost sure of it."

Excitement pulsed through her veins. She'd forgotten this part of police work, the thrill when everything started to come together, or even when a little piece here or there started to make sense. She was on to the killer, had a theory forming in her mind about his motive for committing the murder and everything else.

And if she was right, things were about to get crazy.

TEN

Sawyer hadn't seen Kelsey like this before. Her normally stoic face was knit in an intense frown, but one that looked more like she was thinking than angry, and she was pacing.

He'd called the police four minutes ago, not that he was staring down the time on his watch. In a town Treasure Point's size, they should be here at any minute.

There they were.

"They're here, Kels."

She looked up at him, clearly surprised, and he flinched a little—just because he had the tendency to nickname her in his head didn't mean she'd be open to him using it out loud.

But she didn't comment, either positively or negatively, which didn't surprise Sawyer. He could tell that she was on to a lead for the case, and that had her focus right now, to the exclusion of everything else. For someone who'd only been marking time, making money as a police officer years ago, she seemed to have been an awfully good one.

He tucked that thought away to come back to later, and walked over to where Kelsey was just letting the officers in the door. It was O'Dell and Hitchcock. He was glad to see the two of them. Maybe it was from growing up with them and spending so much free time with them in the Georgia woods, sitting by bonfires, dreaming about the future, and driving too fast down muddy dirty roads. Either way, he trusted them to look out for Kelsey more than he'd trust the other officers, even the older ones with more experience.

"Where's the bag?" another voice asked from behind the two men.

"Shiloh." Kelsey smiled. "I'm glad you're here. I touched it already but then got to thinking about what all there could be…"

"So far, whoever is behind this has been pretty uncomplicated. Bullets and underwater attacks aren't exactly subtle. So I'd say the chances of any kind of poison or powder that could harm you are fairly slim."

Sawyer was thankful to hear that. He'd seen Kelsey drop the bag, but hadn't really thought about why she was doing so. He figured it had just been a reaction, not a calculated move.

"I also called in to the station and asked if someone could check out the museum for me, and see if a map had been stolen like I thought," Kelsey continued.

"We heard that on the radio," Hitchcock said. "The officer stationed at the museum went to check."

"I'm heading there right after I get this bag," Shiloh added. "We have a better chance of getting prints off that scene than this, I think. But better safe than sorry." She snapped disposable gloves onto her hands and reached for the bag. "This is it?"

Kelsey nodded. "Yes."

"These pictures were in the bag while you were at the museum earlier?"

Their eyes moved to the dining room table, Sawyer

watched it happen like it was in slow motion, watched their eyebrows rise at the setup. Did they suspect that she was investigating on her own?

"Is this for what you're doing with the insurance?"

"That's why I needed to take the pictures," Kelsey said calmly, not fully answering the question. Sawyer looked away from her, not sure he'd be able to play it as cool, and found himself accidentally looking straight at Clay.

The other man studied him for a minute, eyes slightly narrowed.

Sawyer was pretty sure Clay wasn't buying it.

"I'm going to need to take them with me to process them for prints." Shiloh moved toward the bag. "I'll be in touch if I find anything. You can probably have the bag back tomorrow or the next day, assuming it's clean. I don't have a lot on my plate right now, so I'll rush this."

"Thank you."

Shiloh nodded, then headed out the door.

"Now, can you tell us again what happened, Kelsey?" Clay asked. "How did you notice that your things had been tampered with?"

"I had laid the pictures out on the table and noticed that one of the photos I'd taken was missing. That's when I figured out that when I hid in the closet after realizing someone was in the museum with me, my bag was still out in the room beside the desk, in plain sight."

O'Dell's cell phone rang. "One minute," he said to Kelsey, and walked away. "Hello?"

Sawyer could still hear his voice, but couldn't make out the words as he'd wandered too far away.

Hitchcock speared Sawyer with a look. "I know what the two of you are doing." He kept his voice low. But it didn't seem like a reprimand, not yet. It almost sounded more…

"You know I can't sit on the sidelines, Clay," Kelsey said, voice etched with frustration. "I trust y'all to do your jobs, and I'm not overstepping any legal lines, I promise. So just—"

"Listen. I'm starting to think we might have another leak in the department." There had been a leak in the department before? Sawyer was surprised, but Kelsey just nodded, as if she was already familiar with that story. "Or maybe we've just been bugged… I'm not sure, but I'm suspicious. You looking into things on your own isn't a terrible idea. I'll feed you whatever information I feel like I can."

Kelsey nodded and glanced at Sawyer. He nodded, too.

"We'll do the best we can," she promised Clay.

Footsteps signaled O'Dell's return. "That was Shiloh. She couldn't wait to look in the bag and says she found something in one of the pockets that struck her as odd. It's an envelope, with your name on it, and a necklace inside. Did you put that there?"

"No." Kelsey shook her head. "What necklace?"

"She said it's a feather and an anchor on a chain."

Sawyer looked at Kelsey. Unless he was imagining things, her face was noticeably paler. "What is it?" he asked.

She shook her head. "It's my necklace. But I wore it yesterday, then put it on my bedside table before I went to sleep last night."

Before anyone could say anything, Hitchcock was already headed up the stairs. In silence, they listened to his retreating and returning footsteps.

"It isn't there," he said.

"He was in my house," Kelsey said as her eyes widened. "He was in my house."

"You can't stay here." Sawyer hoped it was obvious, but with Kelsey, he wasn't counting on it.

"I don't have anywhere else to go," she said, but her protest was weak. It didn't seem like she was that convinced herself. And how could she be? The man who wanted her dead had clearly been inside her house, had gotten through whatever security measures she had in place, and she had been unaware of it.

The thought was sobering to Sawyer. When Kelsey had unlocked the door to let them inside tonight, he hadn't thought to check the house for any sign that it had been breached. Foolishly, he'd assumed that since the door was locked and there was no obvious sign of a break-in, all was well.

Clearly that was far from true.

"There's an apartment at the museum," O'Dell said to Hitchcock.

Kelsey frowned. "Why would the museum have an apartment? There's no need for anyone to live on-site."

"The apartment doesn't belong to the museum—it was there before, from when the Hamiltons lived at the plantation house. They converted the space above the garage into an apartment and used to rent it out."

"If it doesn't belong to the museum, then who does it belong to?" Kelsey asked.

Sawyer cleared his throat, looking awkward. "Me, actually. And you're perfectly welcome to use it. But if the guy is already targeting the museum, is it wise for her to be there?"

"He's targeting her already, too. Besides, this way we can increase police presence there and kill two birds—"

"If you don't mind avoiding the word *kill* that would be great," Kelsey interrupted.

"I think that apartment sounds like a pretty good option," Sawyer said to Kelsey. "What do you think?"

Kelsey just nodded. "Whatever you guys think."

Sawyer had never seen her so compliant. Knowing this guy had been inside her house had rattled her. And he understood why—there was something personal in that, almost more malicious than having a gun fired at you. This was becoming more personal, and it was apparent that Kelsey's nightmare might not be over anytime soon.

As for him? He was starting to think he was in over his head. What did he know about investigating?

Nothing. But he knew he wasn't going to leave Kelsey alone.

Kelsey had felt like she was on autopilot ever since the discovery that the killer had been in her house. Was it just the necklace? Or were there other things he had touched? Were there cameras? Bugs? High-tech surveillance seemed far-fetched for Treasure Point, but so did this entire scenario. The town had some crime, but premeditated murders weren't common.

Yet this was really happening. Someone was trying to kill her for what she'd seen the other night, and it appeared that he was inching ever closer to making her demise a reality.

That thought jolted her, put a bit more of the fight back into her veins. That wasn't going to happen, she wasn't going to let it.

"I need to pack. Can y'all stay while I do?" she asked the officers, who agreed quickly. She started up the stairs, but hesitated halfway up. Both Matt and Sawyer started up the stairs.

"I'll come make sure I don't see anything else suspicious," Matt said.

"I'll keep you company." Sawyer grinned, that easy, laid-back, good-old-boy smile, and Kelsey almost relaxed.

Almost, but not quite. Her life was still on the line.

But it was nice to have Sawyer's smile right here, ready to brighten her day, if only for a second.

"I'll need clothes…" She tried to talk herself through the packing process to hurry it along, but it still took Kelsey more time than she would have liked. In any case, they were headed out the door within half an hour, heading for the museum. Kelsey still hadn't heard whether her suspicions about the map being taken were correct or not.

They pulled up in the museum parking lot and Kelsey eyed the building with the apartment in it—it looked like a carriage house, with a garage area on the bottom and a few windows on the top where she guessed the apartment was. "Is this really okay? This wasn't… Michael wasn't living here, was he?"

Sawyer shook his head. "No, this has been empty since they refurbished it after Aunt Mary moved to the nursing home where her sister lives. It's had electricity this whole time, since it's not wise to turn that off in the South unless you want the whole house to rot in this humidity. I called to have the water turned on while you were packing, so it should be all set."

"I know it's silly, but hearing that it wasn't used by Michael makes me feel better," she muttered. Her situation was creepy and dangerous enough already, she didn't need to add any more by wondering if Michael

Wingate could have left something behind in his apartment that had gotten him killed.

"We'll check it out and then you can get settled. There will be an officer here at all times, maybe two. It's already been cleared with the chief and the museum board," Hitchcock said.

Kelsey nodded. "Thanks." Though she wondered how secure the police presence would really make her if there was a mole or something in the police department.

But he smiled at her a little. "Relax. I'm being careful," he said in a low voice, then started up the outside stairs to the apartment.

Kelsey took a deep breath and followed him, with Sawyer on her heels, which she was grateful for. The man seemed to be sticking to her like glue ever since the scare earlier at the museum. She didn't particularly mind him hovering. All things considered, it probably wasn't a bad idea to have another set of eyes watching her back.

Kelsey waited on the top landing for Clay to finish checking everything out. Standing in the glow of the floodlights on the side of the building made her feel uncomfortable, but she reminded herself that they'd just made the decision to come here so it wasn't as if someone could be lying in wait.

"Everything looks good."

"Good." She walked inside and surveyed the small apartment. There was a kitchen directly inside, with a small table and chairs, and a large living area with a door off the far end. Bedroom and bathroom? It was clear that the place hadn't been occupied in a while—she could see the dust—but other than that, it looked comfortable.

"Thank you for letting me stay here," she said to Sawyer. "I appreciate it."

"I'm glad I could help."

"Oh," Clay said. "Shiloh told me that you were right. The officer on duty phoned into the station and said that the map was missing from the museum." He hesitated. "Whatever you're doing, you're onto something, which is good, but you know it makes your situation more dangerous. Be careful."

"I'm trying," she said.

He nodded. "We'll have someone watching all night, Kelsey. Stay safe."

Then he was gone and Kelsey turned to Sawyer. "If that map is what the killer decided to steal, something not even related to the antiques and artifacts I was photographing, what are the chances that you're right and that something in that room *did* get Michael Wingate killed?"

"The map?" Sawyer asked as he followed her into the living room. She sank down onto the couch, feeling stunned by what she'd managed to think through. He sat beside her.

"Yes. The map."

"You think the guy behind all this wanted it?"

"Or wanted it gone. If he just wanted the image, he could have taken a picture. But if he wanted it destroyed…maybe that's why he killed Michael."

"Just because he'd seen it? That doesn't make sense. He'd have had to kill more people than that, and no one else has had threats made against them."

"True. But what if Michael started to suspect something—made an innocent comment, and the murderer knew he was onto whatever it is the killer is trying to hide?"

"We still don't know what he could be involved in," Sawyer reminded her.

Kelsey laughed, the tension from the night needing

a release. "Sure we do. It's simple. That map? It was the key to someone's treasure. And he didn't want anyone else to find it. Don't you think a criminal might think *that* was worth killing for?"

"I think that Clay's right and you may be onto something. Did you back your pictures up on a computer or anything?"

"They're on my iPad, but it's in the bag. Shiloh has it as evidence right now." Yet another thing that would slow this case down and make her stay in this town longer. It was starting to feel like someone was conspiring against her.

"So they should be in the cloud."

Before he'd finished talking, Kelsey was tapping at the screen of her phone.

There it was, the shaded map with approximations of where several shipwrecks were believed to be.

"You said you scuba dive, didn't you?" Kelsey asked Sawyer without looking up from her phone's screen.

"Of course. Why?" She didn't answer immediately. Understanding gradually dawned. "You're not…"

"It's the only way to find anything else out," she said.

"Okay, now I know that's not true. You could talk to people, do some research, look in some of those books of my grandparents' that I mentioned…"

"Sure, but none of that is going to substitute for being there. We need to figure out *how* these potential shipwrecks play into this now that we know that they do. Is someone planning to find those wrecks for himself? Maybe that exhibit gave them an idea and now they're planning to go search for things."

Kelsey stood and walked the length of the room, then came back.

"What?" Sawyer asked.

"Maybe someone is planning to find the wrecks, or… what if they already did?"

"What do you mean?"

"No one has been interested in Treasure Point history for years. It was only a few years ago when that pirate treasure was discovered that people really started to look back at our history. That's when the museum idea became a reality." Kelsey had never been more glad she'd kept up on some of the town happenings.

"Can you sit back down? You're making me nervous."

Something in Sawyer's voice caught her attention. Kelsey sat down beside him, where she'd been sitting earlier, and then looked over at him. "What's wrong?"

"Seriously?"

"I mean, besides…" She struggled to find words to put there. Besides the fact that someone was trying to kill her? Besides the harsh reality that she had to stay in a house that wasn't hers because the security of her home had been breached? Besides the way that every time they uncovered a layer of what might be behind the villain they were chasing, they discovered another five layers beneath it?

"All of it, Kelsey. It's just really sinking in tonight. This isn't pretend, it's not some show we're watching on TV knowing that series has to continue and that the people in the show are going to make it out alive. It's real life. *Your* life."

"Yours, too." A flicker of guilt twinged in her midsection. "It's probably dangerous for you to be around me."

"Like I'm going to let you do this on your own?" He raised his eyebrows.

"But why, Sawyer? We hadn't spoken in years. Why do you care so much?"

ELEVEN

Sawyer didn't think he could answer the question himself. He looked back at Kelsey and shrugged. "I don't know, but I do."

If the tension in the room had been thick before, it was almost tangible now, but Sawyer made himself hold eye contact with her. He'd meant what he said, wasn't ashamed of it.

Kelsey looked away, as he'd known she would. Even though Sawyer had only meant the comment in a just-friends capacity, he had known even that would make Kelsey uncomfortable. Why was she so resistant to depending on people, to letting others get close to her? He may never find the answers, but he still wanted to figure out how to get her to make an exception for him, to let him become her real friend.

"Okay, then. So the map... What if someone found the ships already and they want to keep them a secret?"

"Why would they want to do that?"

She shook her head. "So they can keep all the treasure to themselves? Or maybe there's something else I'm not seeing. Figuring out people's motives is almost impossible. It's all conjecture. But if I had to guess, I'd say there's a good chance someone has been stealing from the shipwrecks, maybe selling things?"

"So, you think maybe someone destroyed the map, committed murder, tried to kill you and may be trying to sabotage the museum opening because they're plundering shipwrecks and don't want to be found out?"

"It makes just as much sense as anything else. Don't you see?"

Sawyer did understand her point. "How would you prove this? The police have worked the crime scenes and still haven't found anything. Not even prints—the guy who's after you has been extremely careful so far."

"He'll slip up eventually. For now we'll focus on building a case against him, even a circumstantial one is better than nothing because we can use what we're learning, as unofficial as it is, to hopefully catch him in the act or get our hands on concrete evidence."

"And you want to do that by going diving at the wrecks."

"Yes."

"It's not a bad idea," Sawyer finally admitted.

"Really? So you're in? I mean, I know you don't have to come. I've appreciated your help, but I can handle it on my own."

There she went again with the I-don't-need-anyone bit. Sawyer *wanted* to help. How long was it going to take to get her to believe that?

"I want to go."

"Then let's talk about a plan."

It was past midnight when Sawyer slipped back into his parents' house, where he was staying while he took care of the museum business and tried to figure out where he was putting down roots. His résumé was with several prestigious research centers across the Southeast, but in truth he wasn't disappointed about not having heard from any of them yet. Being back in Treasure Point had reminded him of how much the town meant to him. He'd already started looking into the few nearby marine biology job postings he'd found online. Maybe he could live in Treasure Point and commute to work. He was starting to want to stay.

Or maybe that had more to do with his high school class's valedictorian—Kelsey—and less to do with the town itself.

He shut the door behind himself and turned to head for the stairs.

"You're home late."

His dad's voice stopped him in his tracks. Sawyer put his shoulders back, almost unconsciously, and turned to face the older man. "Yes, sir."

"Have you given any more thought to coming back to the company?"

"Dad…" It was too late at night for this conversation, too late altogether.

"It's what you were raised for, Sawyer. Not for chasing some crazy idea of doing something different entirely."

"Marine biology is a respectable field, Dad."

"And you think you're just going to find a job as easy as that?" His dad's laugh had no humor. "Come back to working for me."

"I don't really want to talk about this tonight." Sawyer was impressed with his own ability to stay relatively calm.

"Fine, we'll talk about something else. I've barely seen you since you've been home. What were you up to tonight?"

"I was just out."

"On a date?"

"No, sir."

"I know. I just wanted to see what you'd say. Kelsey Jackson is trouble, Sawyer."

Sawyer pictured Kelsey's slight frame, her sweet smile. Oh, yeah, she was trouble personified. Except not at all. He laughed a little. "I think that's overstating things a little, Dad."

"Not where my son is concerned."

Everything about his dad's body language showed how serious he was. Sawyer shook his head. "She's a friend from high school who's in trouble. I'm just giving her a little bit of help."

"It's not your job to do that."

True, it was the Treasure Point Police Department's, but they were understaffed and Kelsey probably would have refused personal protection from them even if they'd offered it. The woman was frustratingly stubborn, but at least she was letting him help her, be another set of eyes. The unofficial backup to her unofficial investigation.

"It's not. But it's a nice thing to do."

"Sawyer, you need to remember you're different from other people in this town."

Not this speech again. He couldn't picture his Aunt Mary ever saying such things, and his grandparents never would have, either. The Hamiltons had always been a fixture in Treasure Point, and a wealthy one at that, but his parents were the ones who had been determined to turn them into some sort of Southern aristocracy. Maybe Kelsey was right to view them the way she did—he just hadn't wanted her to be.

Sawyer argued back, "We're only different in the

sense that our family has been here forever and may have some more responsibilities to the town, like showing up at these museum events and speaking." He half hoped that referencing those duties would go a little way to making peace with his dad, just to remind him that he was *here* in town for the purpose of doing those sorts of family things.

"That's not all I mean."

So much for trying to give his dad the benefit of the doubt.

Before Sawyer could think of any sort of appropriate reply, his dad spoke up again. "She's not our type of people, son. You've seen her house. Simple. She'd have no idea how to handle the sort of responsibilities that come naturally to you."

"Well, we've seen how I handle those, haven't we?" Sawyer knew his dad would catch the reference to his last business deal, the one he'd tried to do his own way that had gone up in smoke.

"You can do better. She can't. She is who she is."

Weren't they all? And yet, wasn't God capable of using the parts of who they were that He wanted to use to accomplish his purposes in them? And didn't He help them change the parts that needed to be different?

"I'm not having this conversation, Dad. It's ridiculous—first, because Kelsey is perfectly worthy of dating whoever she chooses in this town—she's probably a better person than I am. And second, because I am *not* dating her. I am helping her out, being a friend. That is all." Sawyer shook his head, wishing that staying and talking would work anything out, but knowing that it wouldn't. Rather than try for no reason, he turned back to the stairs and headed up. No wonder Kelsey had something against their family. His parents hadn't been quite this bad when he was in high school, had they? If they'd gotten worse once he'd left for college and she'd had some sort of run-in with them and they'd treated her this way, he didn't blame her at all for wanting nothing to do with him.

Too bad he was starting to care so much about her.

The sunlight streaming through the windows somehow made the day feel more positive to Kelsey. Through the blinds, which she kept mostly closed for safety purposes, she could see snatches of deep blue sky, the shade of blue that only seemed to exist on a perfect summer day.

It was a good day to dive.

Sawyer had told her he had his own equipment, but since her equipment was at her place in Savannah, she needed to rent from a dive shop near the beach. Kelsey didn't love how obvious that made their investigation—it would take very little effort for the killer to discover they'd been exploring out in the ocean, and from there make the leap to realizing they were investigating those shipwreck areas. But there was no way around it.

Kelsey had been just about to make a list when a knock at the door interrupted her. Her heartbeat immediately ratcheted up from where it had been, and she moved to the dresser where she'd locked her handgun in a small portable safe, and moved it to a holster at her waist.

She wasn't taking chances.

"Who is it?" she asked when she was sure her words would sound steady enough.

"Sawyer. Sorry, I should have texted first."

Kelsey smiled and opened the door. "Good morning!

I'm not quite ready yet, didn't we say eight?" It wasn't quite seven.

"Eight is good. I just didn't figure there would be any coffee here, so I brought you some."

"Thanks." She could live without breakfast, but a day without coffee? Not an idea she wanted to consider. Not when she was sure today was not going to be a lot calmer than yesterday or the day before.

She took a sip. "So good. Really, thanks. Do you want to come in?"

He shook his head. "Nah, I don't want to get in the way of you getting ready."

"Do you have more things to do at home?" She eyed his board shorts and T-shirt. He looked ready to her.

"I'm good, but really, I didn't meant to interrupt your morning."

"Just come in." Kelsey laughed.

He stepped inside. She locked the door behind him and put her gun back in the safe. "I'll admit, the knock on the door so early had me a little jumpy."

"Can't blame you."

"So—" Kelsey paused, took another drink of coffee "—are you a talker in the morning or more quiet?"

The grin he gave her was distinctly sleepy. "I could use a little bit of quiet."

She nodded. "Works for me."

Kelsey continued moving around the apartment in silence, drinking the rest of her coffee, then reading a quick chapter from her Bible before digging through the suitcase she'd packed for her swimsuit and something she could wear over it until they got to the rental place and put wetsuits on. Sawyer appeared to be asleep on the couch, leaving her alone with her thoughts.

She let her mind run through all the things overwhelming it at the moment. There wasn't much to work through with the case—she already felt they were making good progress, and there wouldn't be much else they could figure out until they took the next step, which in this case meant investigating some of the shipwreck areas today.

On the subject of Sawyer... Well, she didn't know what to think there. All Kelsey knew was that ever since she'd admitted why she'd been holding a grudge all these years, it seemed God had started freeing her from the anger attached to the loss of the scholarship. In fact, she was seeing through the experience with this investigation that there might have been some hidden blessings in that. What if she'd found herself in this situation and she *didn't* have the knowledge or training to protect herself and help with this case?

It was funny how things worked out sometimes. Kelsey just needed to keep reminding herself of that.

She glanced at her watch. Seven thirty. They could always leave early. The rental shop opened at seven in the most heavy tourist months.

She put on a little waterproof mascara and then went back to the living room. Sawyer was awake now.

"What do you think about leaving early?" she asked him.

"Sounds good to me. I figured we'd head straight to the rental shop to pick up our gear so we don't risk them being out of something, and then grab breakfast."

"Breakfast?" That hadn't been in the plan. And, as much one-on-one time as they'd spent together over these last few days, Kelsey and Sawyer hadn't eaten at a restaurant together. Somehow that thought intimidated her a little bit, like if they did this it would be almost like a real date...

Which was something Kelsey couldn't let herself imagine, even when she had trouble looking away from Sawyer's light eyes that were always sparkling. That look he usually had—like they shared some sort of inside joke—she was actually starting to like it. Instead of seeing it as arrogance, which she abhorred, it was beginning to look more like confidence and genuine friendliness.

"Kelsey?"

He was raising his eyebrows and Kelsey realized she hadn't answered him.

"Breakfast would be good."

Kelsey grabbed a duffel bag with things she thought she might need, including her gun, and they went outside, making sure to carefully lock the door behind them.

"Morning!" They waved to Lieutenant Davies and Officer Dalton, a newer officer—though not as new as Officer Ryan—who were apparently on duty that morning.

"Will they think it's odd we're dressed for the beach when I'm supposed to be trying to stay safe? I mean, they won't suspect that we're going diving to investigate, right?" Kelsey looked to Sawyer for reassurance. He was already nodding.

"I think they don't suspect anything."

They drove straight to the dive shop and told them what Kelsey needed. The worker went to the back to retrieve the gear and Kelsey noticed it seemed to take an unusually long time, longer than it had ever taken before. She thought it was odd and was just about to say something to Sawyer when the man returned with the gear and apologized for the wait. They took the equipment, loaded it into the back of the truck with Sawyer's gear and put the cover back down on the truck bed. Scuba equipment wasn't cheap, so it wasn't uncommon for it to be stolen—sort of like bicycles in other places.

"You know…" Kelsey started, "I really don't need breakfast. I can have a big lunch when we get back." All of that was true, but the real truth was that she was getting entirely too comfortable around Sawyer Hamilton. Going to breakfast with him would only make that worse.

"Whatever you want."

Did he have to be so easygoing and nice?

They hadn't been back in the truck for more than a minute when Kelsey's stomach growled loudly.

"That doesn't sound like you can wait." He laughed. "Let's stop and get something for you to eat."

"No, don't worry about it." Kelsey knew she shouldn't argue. She was being beyond foolish—diving on an empty stomach wasn't something that ever worked well for her. But she couldn't shake the mix of nervousness and discomfort she felt at the idea of going out to eat with Sawyer.

"Let's just go eat and then we'll get out there," Sawyer said. "There's plenty of day. Besides, this way we make sure we're late enough that all the fishermen have left from the docks, and don't see us leaving and ask questions."

"I hadn't thought of that. Do you think I should have?"

"Nah. Even if people see us, they won't think we're investigating because it can always look like…"

Like a date. Kelsey nodded. "Oh, yeah, I get it."

"Not that it…"

"No, of course."

"Not that I…"

"Let's go get some breakfast, okay?" Kelsey nodded. "Breakfast would be great."

Anything to distract them both from this awkward conversation, and even more importantly, from the feelings simmering just beneath the surface in her—and presumably him, too—that were causing it.

"So where did you want to get breakfast?" she asked, ready to change the subject.

"Where else?"

"Stephens Crossing?"

The old diner-style restaurant was a few minutes outside Treasure Point, but it served the best biscuits in all of southern Georgia, and that was quite a title since good biscuits were far from rare here. It had been a favorite hangout of Kelsey's back in high school and during her years on the police force. She wouldn't have expected Sawyer to have spent much time there, but now that she thought of it, she might have seen him there before.

"Sounds great." And like a blast from the past. This could work in her favor. Even though Kelsey was relieved not to have any more bitterness about what had happened in high school, maybe going back to a place associated with that time would remind her that this feeling of closeness she felt with him now was new, and it was just because of the case. Nothing lasting.

Kelsey reached to turn the air conditioner down—it was getting too cold—and as she did so, so did Sawyer. Their fingers brushed and she shivered.

Yeah, nothing lasting. In fact, nothing at all.

She spent most of the drive looking out the window, reminding herself of how close she was to achieving everything she'd set out to do in her career. She would have to travel—that was half of what appealed to her about the job—and Sawyer wasn't the kind of man who'd want a relationship with someone who was never around.

"I don't think you've told me what's next for you, have you?" Kelsey asked, keeping her tone light.

"After this case is solved?"

"Well, that, or just after you're done with your family obligations here."

"I'm looking into jobs using the degree I care about. I sent a couple of résumés out to aquariums, research facilities, places like that, in South Carolina, Georgia and Florida."

"Florida?" Kelsey laughed. "How would you handle that during football season?" Like her and most Georgians, the loyalty to the University of Georgia Bulldogs ran deep, and the Florida Gators were among their more hated opponents.

Sawyer laughed, too, and shook his head. "It'd be tough, but I've got to take what I can find, I guess. We're at the age now to be working our way up in our jobs, right? We can be pickier about our location later."

Kelsey smiled, but quickly looked away from him. Working their way up in their jobs, yes. She needed to repeat that over and over to herself as a mantra. Because the longer she worked closely with Sawyer, the more she wasn't just afraid of danger for her life. She was afraid of it for her heart—and the ten-year plan to which she held so tightly.

TWELVE

With the breakfast debate settled, Sawyer drove his truck in the direction of the best breakfast in the state. He kept his eyes on the road and off Kelsey, because the way she'd smiled at him shyly earlier…

Suddenly he didn't think he was the only one to whom this felt…well, a little like a date.

Except today wasn't about dating, Sawyer reminded himself as he drove. Today was about this gut feeling of Kelsey's. Personally, it felt a bit like a wild goose chase to him, pursuing *rumored* locations of ships that had sunk and were *rumored* to have items of some value on board. If he were the one running this very unofficial show, he would look at those books, see if nosing around through someone else's research would help. Why get out in the field for information someone else might have already found for you?

He sounded like his dad, pushing for safe action, wanting to step back and minimize the risk. The realization bothered him. He sounded like the kind of business man he'd been—the kind of businessman his father had always wanted him to be—before he'd lost the Pellerno deal in the grandest catastrophe of his short career. A marine biologist, in contrast, knew it was important to be hands on, to get information right from the source.

Sawyer thought about his applications, partially completed employment profiles online. Maybe today was important for him, too, to brush up on his investigation skills. Marine biology was a science, but also an art form with a bit of detective work thrown in, just underwater.

"So today should be right up your alley, huh?"

Kelsey broke into his thoughts, almost literally it seemed. He turned and attempted a smile, though his line of thinking was still bothering him a little.

"Yeah, it should be."

"Have you worked marine biology jobs before, or will this be your first?"

Will. Sawyer liked her casual confidence, like there was no doubt in her mind that he could do this. The talk with his dad last night still haunted him. This *wasn't* what he'd been trained to do for the majority of his life. Maybe it was arrogant to expect that a degree and a little experience—the field work required for his degree— would help him break into what was a competitive career in this part of the country.

"If I get a marine biology job, it will be my first."

"Oh, of course you'll be able to get a job. Come on, like everything you've ever touched hasn't turned to gold?"

Yeah, everything he'd touched *with* his dad's blessing. The Pellerno deal had been his dad's idea, but Sawyer's approach hadn't matched his father's, and he'd managed to convince the other man to let him do it his own way, confident he'd be able to impress his dad with his business skills.

If it hadn't flipped his whole life upside down, disappointed his dad, landed him back in Treasure Point on this Hamilton Obligation Tour, Sawyer would laugh. See where confidence had gotten him?

"Yeah, not exactly. So, you know the coordinates you want to check?" he asked Kelsey, hoping the change in subject would stick.

She looked at him for a moment, eyes curious, before she answered. "Yes, I do."

"So we need enough air to be gone all day, right? That's what I got us at the dive shop because I guessed it'll be a pretty long trip."

"Yes, there's no telling how long it will take. If we find things, we might need to stick around underwater longer. Better to be prepared."

"Say we do find something. What does our situation look like then?"

Kelsey seemed to be weighing her options. "I would say it depends on the scale of what we find. If there's a reason to notify the police immediately, we can call them from the boat and wait until they arrive. If we find something small, or something that just seems strange or out of place, we can go home and do some research."

"You don't think you'll get any kind of reprimand?"

She laughed. "For what? I'm not an officer, Sawyer. I'm just a private citizen, who's planning a day of scuba diving off public shores."

"You know it's more than that."

She shrugged. "Sure. You're right. But I also know we aren't doing anything even tending toward ethically wrong."

"I just hope this goes well."

"It will." Kelsey said it with a smile, and Sawyer did all he could to believe her as he put the car in Park at the restaurant.

Stepping into the Stephens Crossing was like coming home—more so than returning to his parents' cavernous house had been.

He looked over at Kelsey and the smile on her face said she felt it, too.

"I love it here," she said with a deep inhale of the air, which was saturated with the smell of biscuits, butter and bacon. "Do you think I could just stay here while we finish investigating? I'm sure I could make a bed in a booth and just eat this food every day..."

Sawyer laughed. "You go ahead and ask them. Let me know how it goes."

To Sawyer's surprise, breakfast hadn't been the least bit uncomfortable. After that odd exchange in the car, he'd been a little nervous about the possible turns the conversation could take.

But Kelsey steered their conversation clear of anything too personal. That woman was socially adept, for sure. He didn't understand why she'd chosen a job that limited her interactions with people so much, even if she was good with antiques. It seemed a bit odd, but he didn't really know her well enough to ask her about something so personal. After all, when Sawyer hadn't wanted to talk any more about his career choices earlier, Kelsey had respected that. He owed her the same courtesy.

Kelsey's phone rang just as they reached the truck and were preparing to unload their gear and carry it the hundred yards between downtown and his boat, which was at Treasure Point's main dock.

"Hello?" she answered, walking away a little as she did so.

"Really?" she said, a minute later.

She was too far away to hear now, so Sawyer worked on unloading the scuba gear and tried to keep a close eye on her. He'd like to think no one would attack her downtown in broad daylight, but stranger things had happened.

Kelsey walked back, phone in her hand. "That was Shiloh. She says I can come get my stuff back anytime."

"Do you need to do that and get back to work?" He wasn't sure how deadlines worked in jobs like hers.

"We need to do this and we're ready and my gear is rented, so we may as well go ahead." She said it without hesitation. "Even though it does feel a little bit like playing hooky."

Sawyer understood that. The sky was bright blue, the sun was shining and it would be so easy to forget everything that had been happening and just enjoy the summer day.

Except the threat against Kelsey's life was like a storm cloud closing in on them, one that it would be foolish to ignore.

"Which boat is yours?" Kelsey asked as they walked toward the docks.

He watched her scan the boat slips, and wondered what she was thinking, which one she was assuming was his. He'd guess she'd pegged one of the larger ones, but instead he led her to a modest diving boat. At twenty-six feet, it wasn't small, but it wasn't fancy. It did the job well and would serve him well when he got a job.

"I like it." She turned to him with a smile and he tried to ignore the burst of warmth he felt at her approval.

They climbed onto the boat, the familiar back and forth of the craft on the ocean swells making Sawyer more at ease immediately. He'd always felt like this on the ocean, like he finally fit somewhere. It was what had drawn him to marine biology initially—the desire to find a legitimate career that would allow him to spend most of his days on the water.

Too bad he still hadn't managed to sell his dad on the idea. At least he knew where he stood, knew there was no point in trying to make him proud on a professional level.

On a personal level, though, Sawyer still held out hope. Obviously, or he wouldn't be in Treasure Point right now.

He pulled in the buoys, untied the boat from the dock cleats and tossed the loose ends of the ropes onto the deck of the boat. He then maneuvered out of his slip and onto the waters of the Atlantic.

He said nothing as they headed due east to the open ocean. The swells increased in height as they drew farther from the shore.

"It's cooler out here on the water," Kelsey commented.

Sawyer nodded. "It is. It's another world out here." Usually that brought him comfort, but today he had an odd feeling of uncertainty, the ocean not offering its usual solace. Sawyer couldn't get the threat against Kelsey's life off his mind. Wasn't she safer out here? No one could hide and try to shoot at her, no one could come on their boat without his knowing…could they?

Why can't I shake this, God? Help me to calm down and trust if I'm supposed to. Otherwise, help me figure out how to keep her safe.

It wasn't long before they reached the first set of coordinates they planned to investigate.

He stopped the boat.

Kelsey shook her head. "Not here."

"Why?"

"This is the site closest to Treasure Point. I think there's a bigger chance that *if* anyone already knows about these wrecks and has explored them, they would have started with the most secluded first."

Sawyer sat back down. "Are you sure?" He eyed the clouds gathering in the distance, threatening from far away across the mostly blue sky. "We probably won't be able to spend all day out."

Kelsey frowned. "Maybe you're right."

"Hey, you're in charge. We'll go with whatever you think."

The way she hesitated made it seem like she was fighting a bigger battle than he could see. It shouldn't be a big deal, should it? Either she trusted her first instinct or not. But she seemed to be wrestling with whether or not she should.

"No, let's stay here."

"All right." Sawyer went through the familiar motions of suiting up for the dive and Kelsey did the same. The easy way she prepared showed she'd been scuba diving more than she'd let on.

They both dropped into the water a few minutes later and started to swim.

Visibility was worse than Sawyer had anticipated at the surface, a fact that he hoped wouldn't stop them from finding some useful information for Kelsey. She was counting on today to turn the tables in their favor, he could tell. And in a way, he felt responsible for the day's success, since he was the one with the boat, the one who'd arbitrarily chosen this first dive location.

He could only hope he hadn't chosen wrong. Kelsey wasn't the only one second-guessing instincts.

He motioned to Kelsey to stay close and she nodded. Scuba diving was always safer with a buddy—you never knew what could go wrong underwater, and there were too many scenarios to take the chance of being alone if anything happened.

Sawyer gently took himself deeper into the ocean and Kelsey followed. Visibility improved the deeper they got, since the water wasn't being churned by the wind. That was the good news. The bad news was that there was nothing directly under them. It made sense that there wasn't—they'd randomly picked coordinates in the middle of the shaded zone on the map, so it was logical that a little work would be required to find anything—provided there was something there at all. But…

They might have picked a good random spot. Off in the distance, not too many yards away, he could vaguely make out a large dark shape that must have been a downed ship. He motioned to Kelsey and they swam toward it. When they got there, they discovered that there truly was a boat resting on the ocean floor. He could vaguely make out the letters of the name on the side. This one was *The Determination*. He'd read about it when he'd done some research on the rumored sunken ships last night. *The Determination* was a cargo ship that had been taken over by pirates and then used up and down the Eastern Seaboard until it sank in 1709, just a few years before Blackbeard had sunk his own most prized ship off the coast of North Carolina.

Kelsey tapped his arm, motioned to the ship. Sawyer hesitated. He didn't mind getting closer to it, but if Kelsey was hoping to explore the dilapidated rooms of the ship to see if any artifacts were still there, he'd prefer to have better visibility. Apparently he'd gotten spoiled in all the trips he's taken to Florida, where the water was crystal clear in so many places.

Here in Georgia, the peculiar dark green hue of the water was only broken up by the limited yellow rays of the sun still visible this far down. The sun provided enough light to get around, but to see details, they'd need Sawyer's LED flashlight. Sawyer moved the flashlight's beam from left to right, scanning the back of the ship the best that he could. It had become an artificial reef, as many wrecks did. Growth on the ship itself had softened it, made it part of the ocean landscape, and there were plenty of animals using it as a home.

They circled the wreck carefully, with Sawyer taking mental notes of what he saw. One loggerhead turtle swam away off the starboard side of the boat and Sawyer wished he had his underwater camera with him, even though this wasn't a pleasure expedition. As soon as the thought crossed his mind he was frustrated with himself for not thinking of it earlier. Of course they should have brought a camera. It was a big detail that had slipped his mind.

Like she could read his mind, Kelsey held up a camera and gave him a thumbs-up sign. Sawyer exhaled his relief, then reminded himself again to be conscious about keeping his breathing steady. They should have plenty of oxygen for this dive, but it was never a good idea to get careless and start breathing too abnormally.

They finished their circle of the wreck, admiring the fish and the one nurse shark they saw. Nothing on the outside implied anyone had been here. As far as Sawyer could tell, the wreck was untouched by anything except time and marine life.

There was nothing left to do here but go inside. Sawyer motioned to the opening to Kelsey and she nodded. She headed that direction, and Sawyer followed. He hadn't done any diving inside shipwrecks before, but he imagined that the skills and cautions were the same as those used in cave diving, which he'd done plenty of in the last few years. Had Kelsey? He hadn't thought to ask her earlier, although he probably should have. The way she moved underwater, though, he was fairly certain she had plenty of experience. Everyone had a specific style when they swam and dove, and Kelsey's was boldness with some grace about it. It was so Kelsey that he smiled.

Keeping his breathing even and steady, he followed her inside the ship. The risk inherent in this whole expedition hit him again—diving well took time, and there was a chance they'd spend their entire day at this wreck and not find anything useful to their case. Would it still be helpful to their investigation? Sawyer wasn't sure, but they were here now, so they might as well explore. Kelsey apparently agreed with his unvoiced decision. She kept swimming in front of him, clearly hopeful that they'd manage to find something—or better yet, find a *lack* of objects that should have been with the ship—to indicate whether or not someone had been plundering here or not.

They entered the wreck through a broken spot on the side and came into a room that was empty. There seemed to be nothing inside except for some fish swimming around. Kelsey snapped a picture.

They continued through the wreck, finding much of the same—lots of marine life, but no artifacts. Was it possible that all of the smaller articles had been dispersed by the ocean over time, that they'd been lost to currents and the natural process of decay, and not to plunderers?

Kelsey stopped on the edge of another cabin, then carefully used her arms to sink lower, almost to the floor of the wreck. She snapped a picture of something, then motioned to Sawyer to come closer. A modern, untarnished dive knife lay on the sand.

They weren't the first ones to find this wreck.

It still didn't say for sure that anyone had stolen things from it, but it could mean that. It was more evidence than they'd had up until this point.

They finished their exploration of the ship and headed back toward the outside. Sawyer had started to feel claustrophobic, but he was encouraged by what they'd found today, even if it wasn't much. Kelsey was holding the camera in one hand, the dive knife in the other.

They'd just exited the ship when Kelsey's swimming pattern changed. First she paddled harder in the water, looking almost…frantic? The things she'd been holding fell from her hands, but she made no move to swim after them, instead making frantic motions toward her pressure gauge.

Sawyer looked at the gauge.

It was squarely in the red zone.

How?

It didn't matter how. They had to surface—but despite the urgency, they couldn't go up too quickly. Ascending required significantly more time than descending into the water, because if a diver rose too fast, they could die from the bends.

He handed her his extra regulator from the octopus rig on his back and she inhaled. Exhaled. He wasn't surprised to note that she was breathing too fast, panic did that. He held up a hand, motioned for her to calm down. Her breathing slowed. They swam slowly to the surface. She should be okay.

Thirty feet.

Twenty feet.

Ten feet. They should be okay.
Five feet.
And Kelsey went limp in his arms.

THIRTEEN

Kelsey opened her eyes in a room with a bad nineties' wallpaper border that made her cringe for a moment before she noted the rich, abundant supply of oxygen. The border could be as ugly as it wanted—all she cared about was taking a deep breath. She closed her eyes again, just with the sheer pleasure of being able to breathe.

"I'm alive," she said after another deep breath. Even as she said it, she was running over the incident in her memory. She'd started to feel low on air, checked her regulator and found it dangerously low…too low for the short amount of time they'd spent underwater. Then the headache she'd had since they'd started the dive had started to intensify, almost exponentially, and even Sawyer sharing his air with her hadn't stopped her from passing out.

Everything was disjointed from there, fuzzy. She'd passed out, she was pretty sure. She almost remembered Sawyer's arms around her, but not nearly enough to appreciate it.

Although, in theory, she didn't dislike the concept of his arms around her…

She usually would have pushed the thought away. But now…now she shoved it only slightly aside, let it linger in the corner of her mind, though not in the forefront.

This whole time, she'd been chasing this dream of her career with such purpose, more than happy to let any ideas of romance fall to the side. It was the plan she'd had since high school career class, when they'd learned how to make budgets, how to plan for their career goals and achieve them. Kelsey might have had to work longer and harder than almost anyone she knew, but she was close now, so close to being able to attain those goals she'd set so long ago.

And now she was wondering...

Why did it matter so much if she rose in the world of antiques insurance?

At the time, it had seemed like a prestigious career, and Kelsey had loved history and antiques, so she'd chosen it. When she considered it as her ultimate career choice after high school, while she was working at the police department to make money for college, she'd loved the idea of this job because it didn't involve as much guesswork as law enforcement tended to.

She wouldn't say she felt the same rush working with the Harlowe Company as she had the last few days of investigating. And while it was tempting to say that her job wasn't as dangerous as law enforcement, which was true for the most part. But she wasn't law enforcement right now, and still she'd faced dangers, both from the killer coming after her and just from activities like scuba diving. No, she was an antiques insurance agent, and she was *still* caught up in something dangerous. So there went that argument...

"You're awake."

She looked up and met Sawyer's eyes, her cheeks heating slightly as her thoughts about earlier, about him holding her, came to mind.

"I am, thanks to you, I'm guessing." She gestured to the hospital room. "You brought me here?"

"I called the police department and the ambulance from the boat and met them at the docks. They brought you in."

"Yeah, but you dragged me out of the water, I'm guessing. Thank you."

He nodded. "You're welcome. You scared me, Kelsey."

"I haven't been diving in a while, but I didn't think it had been that long that I didn't remember how to dive safely…" Whatever mistake she'd made, she wasn't sure what it was yet, but Kelsey couldn't believe she'd made it.

"What do you mean?"

"To let my oxygen get so low so fast…" She shook her head.

"Your O-ring was tampered with, Kelsey. I thought so when I saw it, and several of the officers there at the docks agreed with my initial assessment. Shiloh is looking at it now, but that's our guess as to what happened. We're guessing someone followed us to the dive shop, or saw us pull up there and guessed our plans, then tampered with the O-ring at the shop, maybe when the owner or worker wasn't looking. And we also think the mix in your oxygen tank may have been carbon monoxide heavy. Of course, it's empty now, so there's no way prove it." Sawyer's voice betrayed his frustration and anger.

That explained the headache. So, whoever wanted her dead had tried to kill her *again*, this time in a way that would leave no witnesses and no evidence behind except the O-ring itself, which didn't have any forensic evidence that would help them.

"So what now?"

"You have to be observed for a few more hours. After that—" Sawyer lowered his voice "—Clay has asked us to meet with him. We're going to meet at my house."

"Are you staying with your parents?"

He nodded.

Kelsey hoped he couldn't tell that she was cringing, or at least would attribute whatever face she was making to her near-death experience earlier, and not to the idea of being forced into close proximity with his parents.

"Sounds like a plan."

The next few hours passed quickly, and as soon as the doctor gave Kelsey a clean bill of health, and another admonition to be careful when scuba diving—the hospital hadn't been told about the apparent sabotage—Kelsey and Sawyer were out the door and back in his truck.

The drive to Richard and Lori Beth Hamilton's house didn't take nearly as long as Kelsey would have liked. Before long they were pulling up in front of the stately brick house near the marsh.

Kelsey took a deep breath. "Sawyer, here's something you don't know that you need to."

He froze, his hand hovering over the seat belt latch. "Okay. Right now?"

"Before we go in there." She swallowed hard, all the old memories returning, all the reminders of how she'd trusted her gut once and been so horribly wrong, all the weighty feelings of responsibility…

"Did your parents mention to you, sometime when you were away…at college—" she was proud of herself for having come so far that she only slightly stumbled over the word *college* in conversation with him "—that they'd had some criminal activities out here?"

"I've heard rumors here and there, but nothing concrete."

"Anyway, there was. And we had a suspect in custody. But I believed his story over theirs, let him go too soon, and there you go. That was the end of me working for the police department." And it had been a very dramatic conclusion to the one personal interaction she'd had with the Hamiltons, a family she'd never liked much in theory—besides Mary Hamilton—because of how they seemed to act so far above the rest of the town.

"Was leaving the department your choice?"

Kelsey shrugged. "Sort of. I wasn't fired, but there were plenty of people who didn't want me to stay. Choosing to resign seemed like the only option. The chief is very good about supporting his officers, but your parents are powerful people. I don't know how far they would have taken things."

"They weren't happy with you."

She shook her head.

"Look, you made a mistake. People make them."

Kelsey raised her eyebrows and met his eyes. She saw he knew what she was about to say, but said it anyway. "Hamiltons don't. At least, that's what I was told when I offered that excuse. Anyway, I had enough saved to start college by then, so I left and that's what I did."

"And that's the last time you relied on gut instinct."

She shifted in her seat. "Maybe, but that isn't a bad thing. I mean, look at today. I wanted to go somewhere else, farther out to sea. If we'd done that, what if you hadn't been able to get me back to shore and to the hospital in time? It wasn't necessarily a bad thing that I ignored my gut instinct."

"But sometimes you should trust it?"

Kelsey shook her head. "No, I'm not sure about that. It's too uncertain, too much of a risk."

"You've never had a problem with risk."

"That's true. It's not the risk, really. It's the uncertainty. Why rely on something that's suspicion, a feeling, when you could have solid facts behind you?"

"So, do you think that in that case all those years ago—"

Kelsey held up a hand. "Sorry, but it's in the past. There's no need for us to talk about it anymore now. I wouldn't have brought it up at all, but there's a good chance your parents will and I didn't want you to feel like you were out of the loop."

He nodded slowly, though she could tell he wasn't happy about being cut off.

"Well, let's go then."

Kelsey drew in a breath, one more glorious breath of fresh air. Because she might not be back underwater with a broken O-ring and rapidly diminishing oxygen, but facing Sawyer's parents felt disturbingly similar.

Sawyer wished they'd had more time to talk; there were so many things about Kelsey's new personality, the small changes he'd seen in her since high school, that made more sense now that he knew more about her. To think she'd faced off against his parents... He knew all too well how that felt. The difference was that he was their son and they loved him—or at least found him useful—so there was an element of graciousness there that softened the edges a bit.

Kelsey would have had no such softening.

As they approached the door, he had the craziest desire to reach for her hand, somehow assure her that if it came down to any kind of verbal disagreement between her and his parents, he was on her side. He loved his mom and dad, but he knew how they could be, and sometimes that was unusually harsh.

But he knew that reaching for her hand would only cause more problems with the unpredictability of his parents' reaction, and he didn't want to subject her to that, either.

There was nothing about this situation he liked.

He braced himself as slid his key into the door and let them in. "Ready?" he asked Kelsey quietly.

"Doesn't really matter whether I am or not," she said in a voice just as quiet. He did notice that she drew herself up taller, though. A strange swell of admiration made him smile. Kelsey could seem quiet, but she was a fighter.

They made it through the door without incident. In fact, it was so quiet he was wondering if maybe his parents could be out, playing tennis, or on one of their boats…

"Sawyer, is that you?"

He should have known it was too good to be true.

"Yes, Mom. And a friend."

"A friend?"

His mom came around the corner from the kitchen and narrowed her eyes. "I believe we've met, correct? Officer…"

"Just Kelsey, ma'am. Kelsey Jackson."

"You aren't with the police department anymore?" Sawyer recognized his mom's fake innocent look, batting eyelashes and all. She knew full well that Kelsey was no longer a police officer—and she was rubbing it in.

"No, I'm an antiques insurance agent."

"Well, isn't that nice?"

"Mom, Kelsey and I are supposed to be meeting with Clay Hitchcock. You know him, right?"

"Officer Hitchcock? Of course. He's one of the town's finest police officers."

Was it his imagination, or did his mom look to Kelsey a little as she said that?

"Would it be all right if we used the study? We need privacy."

"Of course." She nodded. "Your father is out, but he should be home soon. No need to bother him."

"I won't."

Kelsey was just standing, looking rather frozen in place at the moment, despite her squared shoulders, so he broke his "no contact" rule, put one hand on the small of her back and guided her toward the library. She didn't say anything, but followed his lead.

As soon as they'd entered the room and shut the door, she stepped away from his touch and looked at him with raised eyebrows. "What was that about?"

"You seemed like you needed a little help."

"I was fine on my own."

"You always are, aren't you?" Sawyer exhaled, knowing he'd hear about that gesture from his mom later, and a little disappointed that Kelsey couldn't appreciate the genuine kindness he'd been offering.

He didn't know if she heard him or not, because before either of them could say anything, someone knocked on the door.

"Please tell me that's not your parents," she muttered and pulled a book from the shelf, burying her face in it immediately like it would make her invisible.

It was Clay.

"Come in." Sawyer motioned the other man forward and shut the door behind him.

Clay whistled. "This is impressive. I don't think I ever came here when we were in high school."

Probably not. Sawyer had always preferred to spend his free time away from home.

"Have a seat." Sawyer motioned to her.

"Thanks."

"So, what do we know?" Kelsey asked, clearly unable to contain her excitement about possible progress any longer.

Clay shook his head. "Not a lot, unfortunately. Autopsy results are in on Wingate, and it's definitely homicide. Blunt force trauma to the head caused his fall but there were bruises on his forearms consistent with a struggle before his death, and with someone pushing or throwing him from the balcony."

"Well, we knew he was murdered."

"We *suspected* that. Now we're sure. But we still don't have anything pointing to who did it. Do you have any guesses?"

"As far as who did it? No. But I'm almost positive I have a motive."

"Yeah?"

"That map that was taken from the museum. We're pretty sure it has something to do with the murder."

"We?" Clay glanced at Sawyer.

Sawyer shrugged. "I'm really just here for her to bounce ideas off of. And to make sure no one can surprise her. Tell him, Kelsey."

"You know we spent the day scuba diving."

"Yeah, I heard it almost got you killed. And I admit I was wondering why you'd given up on the investigation for the day to take some time to have fun like that. The old Kelsey was like a bloodhound with a scent when she was on a case."

"Lovely description." Kelsey smiled, though, and Sawyer could tell she actually appreciated the oddly worded praise. "We weren't playing hooky. When we found that map was stolen from the museum, we were pretty sure it had something to do with our case. Sawyer brought up the idea that Wingate was killed in that room for a reason, maybe something there set the killer off."

"Okay, I can understand that."

"And the map was the first thing we thought of."

"It's a map of shipwrecks, right?"

"Yes, but not a very precise one. There are just shaded areas where wrecks are rumored to be. We caught a break today, and didn't have to swim far from the place where we guessed one of the wrecks might be to actually find it."

"That's quite a break."

"We thought so. Anyway, the ship has been overtaken by the ocean, but the odd thing is, we didn't find any sorts of artifacts one might expect to find."

"Such as?"

Kelsey shrugged. "Navigational tools would have been a real coup, but I wasn't counting on those. But there should have been dishes, or at least fragments. Tools… It's hard to say for sure, but what there *shouldn't* be is absolutely nothing."

"So you think someone has been there."

"We know someone has. We found a dive knife. It's modern—definitely not a relic."

"Not yours?"

"No."

"Where is it?"

Kelsey fell silent. Glanced over at Sawyer and shook her head. "I dropped it when I started to feel the effects of the overload of carbon monoxide and ran out of oxygen."

"You dropped your camera, too," Sawyer said. He'd seen them both fall, but there hadn't been anything he could do about them. Getting to Kelsey and helping her get to the surface had been his top priority, and even if he could go back and do it again, her well-being would *remain* his top priority.

"So, if someone is plundering those sites, that's a federal offense. Extremely serious."

"I'm sorry, I just thought of something. I'll be right back." Kelsey slipped out of the room with her phone. Sawyer told himself to remember to ask her later what that was all about.

As soon as she'd left, Clay turned to him, looking more serious. "What do you think, Hamilton?"

"What do you mean?"

"She's my cousin and I want to look out for her, but you're the one who has been spending the most time with her, so you're the one who'll know if she's in over her head. How do you think she's holding up? Do I need to quit encouraging her to keep looking?"

"No, no need for that." Sawyer wanted to defend Kelsey without thinking, but made himself pause and consider the other man's questions. "She's…she's amazing. She might be the best investigator I've ever seen—no offense, man—and when she goes with her instincts it's almost uncanny how she can figure things out. And, yeah, this is all stressful, but I think it helps her to be able to do something, instead of just sitting back and worrying. It makes her feel like she has some control, you know? I'm just… I don't understand who the real Kelsey is. I thought she was methodical, all about facts. And she's struggling with that, I can tell. Sometimes she listens to her gut. Sometimes she doesn't."

Clay shrugged. "She prefers facts. Logic. But when she can let those go, you're right. She's one of the best I've ever seen, too. It's just after she left here, went to school and took that fancy job in Savannah, I wasn't sure she'd still be able to go back to relying on those instincts. But she is?"

"Sometimes."

"Then I can still use her help. This is getting messy in a way that makes it seem like the criminal has an ear in the police department. There are just too many coincidences, too many times, places and opportunities that our bad guy shouldn't have known about. And while I trust everyone in the department—I have to in order to do this job—there are only a few I trust without hesitating. Kelsey makes that list."

The door creaked open again. Kelsey smiled. "Sorry. Where were we?"

"We…" Sawyer looked at Clay. Clay shrugged and Sawyer struggled with what to tell her. His phone rang just as he was about to admit defeat and tell her they'd been talking about how best to keep her safe—a subject he wasn't eager to bring up with her.

Sawyer reached for the phone. "Hold on. I don't know this number."

Everyone stilled and got quiet so he could answer.

"Hello?"

"Sawyer, it's Shiloh Cole. From the police department."

"Shiloh. Hi."

Everyone else in the room relaxed. Sawyer didn't know Shiloh well, but if Clay and Kelsey trusted her, as it appeared they did, then he guessed he could assume she was on their side.

"I'll just get right to it. I need your truck, Sawyer."

"What?"

"I need to borrow your truck and dust it for prints."

"Um…sure. If you need it. But why?"

"Someone tampered with Kelsey's equipment, and I combed the dive shop, but found no evidence. The place was clean. Literally and figuratively speaking. Your truck is my last-ditch effort to find any trace of who's behind it all. This has escalated enough."

"I'll be right there." Shiloh told him where to meet her, and after agreeing and saying goodbye, Sawyer disconnected.

"What was that about?" It was Kelsey who asked, but Clay looked interested, too.

"Shiloh wants to fingerprint my truck, but she asked to meet me in Brunswick instead of at the station here."

"She must suspect something, too…" Clay's voice trailed off.

Sawyer nodded. "Exactly what I thought."

"Maybe she'll find something and give us all a name of who's behind this."

Sawyer could only hope.

FOURTEEN

Kelsey hadn't paid half a second's attention to Sawyer's suggestion that she stay with Clay while he took Shiloh the truck. Instead, she was beside him on I-95, headed into Brunswick.

"So, Shiloh doesn't trust everyone at the police department, either," Kelsey commented, finally breaking the companionable silence that had stretched between the two of them for most of the drive from Treasure Point.

"It doesn't look like it."

"Someone there has got to be working with whoever is behind this, feeding them information. We know it's not her, and not Hitchcock."

"We can rule out O'Dell, too. I'd trust him with my life," Kelsey said. "The chief, too."

"Who does that leave?"

"Officer Ryan, Lieutenant Davies, although he seems unlikely given how long he's been with the department. The other new guys I don't know well are Officer Dalton and Officer Kraft. Then there's always the receptionist."

"Any reason to suspect any of the new officers over the others?"

"No. None."

It was almost more frustrating to be so close and still so far away from finding out who was behind the murder and the attempts on her life. Instead of having any kind of relief from having a pool of suspects, Kelsey was more nervous than ever. Someone with the police department feeding information to a killer? Part of her brain refused to believe it, and Kelsey acknowledged then that at least a few drops of police blood would apparently always be running through her veins in some way, because she couldn't shake the overwhelming feeling of betrayal. An officer?

Still, though, she reminded herself as they turned into the parking lot of the Brunswick Police Department, police officers were only human. There were bad cops just like there were bad teachers, bad retail workers, bad firemen. That didn't make everyone in any profession any more prone to it than another, it just meant that all people were sinful. Besides, at least it wasn't like they were considering one of the officers being the one who kept trying to kill her. It was likely a case of one of them covering for someone, if anything. Maybe the information had even been given innocently—without knowing the killer's true intent. It would still be bad for the officer if it was proven that he'd given out confidential information, but a mistake was easier to forgive than deliberate action.

"There she is." Sawyer laughed a little. "Shiloh looks like she's about to jump out of her own skin."

"Wouldn't you be? She's the only crime scene investigator in Treasure Point, or at least, the only one with her level of certification, and it looks like the work she does might be what solves this. That's a lot of weight on one person's shoulders."

Kelsey understood that.

They parked the truck and climbed out, their doors slammed almost simultaneously as both of them hurried to where Shiloh was waiting right beside the building.

They turned the truck over to her. "I'll be about an hour," she warned them.

Kelsey looked at Clay. "What now?"

"Coffee?"

They walked in the heat until they found the nearest coffee shop, got iced coffees and then started back. Shiloh might not be finished yet, but it was worth checking.

They found her and a few other people at the truck.

"Nothing," she said flatly. "Actually, there are prints all over it, but they're all Kelsey's, and I'm assuming yours. I'll need a print to confirm that. Not a single fingerprint from another person."

"Thanks for trying."

Shiloh nodded, shoulders dropping even lower. "I don't know where to look next." She looked up at Kelsey. "Clay said you were poking into things a little?"

Kelsey hesitated, but then answered honestly. "We are." She braced herself for a lecture, a condemnation of some kind.

"Good," Shiloh said. "Something isn't right about this case. But I don't know what it is yet. We need as many eyes on this as we can get, and from everything I've heard about you, you were one of the best."

Kelsey's cheeks heated a little. "Thanks, Shiloh." She wished, not for the first time, that their tenures at the police department had overlapped instead of them just barely missing each other. Shiloh would have been fun to work with.

Kelsey and Sawyer climbed into the truck. "Back to town?" Sawyer asked.

Kelsey nodded. "Yes."

Her phone rang when they'd been driving for ten minutes or so.

"Hello?" Kelsey said. The number was that of her office back in Savannah.

"Miss Jackson, it's Lacey. You asked me to look for some specific antiques in our database?"

"Yes. Did you find any?"

"There is a navigational tool that came from a ship around the same time period you told me to look for. I thought you might be interested in that. There's also an old sword. It has no solid provenance, but the owners insist it was once owned by a pirate. They were both from the same seller. The owners didn't catch his name—it was a rather informal transaction, outside of an official antiques fair they were all attending. They said they usually wouldn't have paid any attention to someone selling outside of official channels, but the navigational tool seemed more valuable than what he was asking so they decided it was an acceptable gamble."

"All right, thank you, Lacey." Kelsey's heart pounded. Their theory that someone had looted a sunken ship looked correct so far. Now to prove it. "Did they say if there's a ship name or anything inscribed on the navigational tools?" There wasn't always, but Kelsey could hope...

"It's rubbed off."

There went her hope, crashing with the force of an ocean wave on the shore.

"They can read some of the first few letters, though," Lacey continued, obviously wanting to be helpful. "But all they can read is *The Deter*. I'm sorry if that doesn't help much, but I do want you to know that I tried—"

Lacey kept going. The Harlowe Company was notoriously hard to please, at least, Kelsey's bosses and associates were, so she didn't blame Lacey for tripping over herself to be helpful, but Kelsey had stopped hearing her.

The Deter—the first few letters of *The Determination*.

"Thank you, Lacey." Kelsey kept her voice calm, a stark contrast to the wild beating of her heart. "I have go to for now."

"All right, Miss Jackson, I'm sorry I couldn't help more."

Lacey had no idea.

Kelsey hurried back over to where Sawyer was standing. "You're not going to believe this," she said, out of breath.

"What?"

"I called my assistant earlier, when I stepped out of that meeting with Clay, to ask her if she could look into our files for me and see if she could find any artifacts recently bought or sold that might have been from pirate shipwrecks. She came up with a long list—it's a commonly sought-after item in this part of Georgia—but when I had her narrow it down by time period, the one she thought was most important was a navigational tool."

"And you think that proves our theory, that someone found those wrecks and is selling what's in them? Can the tool be tied to one of the wrecks?"

"The engraving is mostly deteriorated. But she can read *The Deter.*"

Sawyer whistled. "I guess we have our motive."

"It's not solid and provable beyond a shadow of a doubt yet," Kelsey said, to remind herself as much as him. "But compared to what we had? This is huge."

"Do you want to look for more wrecks now? Head back out in my boat?"

"I don't know. I'm happy this confirmed our suspicions, but now…"

"What about the library? I promised you a look at those books, and while I don't know exactly how they could help us, there are some that deal with the history of that time period. Is it worth the time it would take to investigate it or is it a dead end?"

Kelsey seemed to consider his question. "I think… that's a good idea. Are they in the study we were in earlier?"

"Some of them. But most of the ones I think have the most promise are in boxes in my parents' attic."

"Let's go unpack them."

The attic was one of the few parts of the house that didn't have his mother's stamp of overdone Southern decor on it. When he'd been younger, he'd loved spending time exploring up there, partly because it was like his own enormous private hideout that his mom wouldn't come into. Too many spiders, she'd say, although Sawyer didn't think he'd seen one spider brave the terrain.

Unlike typical Georgia attics that were used mostly for non-climate-controlled storage, this attic was more like the upper floor of the house, but with slightly lower ceilings and no windows. The walls and rafters were all painted white, though the color had yellowed slightly overtime. Boxes were stacked neatly against the walls and the floor was clean, obviously swept. Someone had been up here lately. Most likely the housekeeper his mother pretended she didn't have.

"They should be in these boxes." Sawyer tugged one away from the wall, opened it up. Old yearbooks. "Okay, not this one."

"What's that?" Kelsey came up behind him. "Yearbooks?"

She pulled the first one off the stack, the one from their senior year of high school. "Lots of signatures in here from girls who were half in love with you, I'd imagine."

"Not hardly."

Kelsey scanned over the pages. "'Have a good summer.' Oh, very creative. 'I'd love to hang out sometime.' And…oh."

She got silent. Sawyer looked at the page she'd read.

There was Kelsey's signature. How had he not noticed before? Sawyer blamed the hustle and bustle of yearbook-signing days, the frantic excited countdown to graduation. But apparently Kelsey Jackson had signed her name in his yearbook.

Right underneath the words "Have fun at college." They sounded innocent. But now that he knew…he could hear the bitterness in them.

She looked up at him. "I'm sorry. I should have handled things better."

"You were seventeen and I stole your scholarship."

"You didn't. You earned it. I know that now." Kelsey looked around the room. "I also know that wishing you had someone else's life…well, it's not really practical, because no one's life is perfect."

"You wished you had my life?" Underneath everything he found out about this woman, there was always another layer waiting to be discovered, wasn't there?

"I mean, not exactly. But to someone whose family never seemed to have any extra money, whose dreams were limited by that, who felt like the world depended on how much money you made…yeah, I envied your lifestyle a little. I always wondered what it must be like to be one of you guys. To not have money factor into any worries at all."

Sawyer didn't comment. Money muddled things in his mind. He'd wished more than once that his family's wealth would disappear—maybe not the best thing to wish for, but it seemed to him that money only complicated their relationships, provided another thing for people to fight about. Something else to put distance between them.

"I'm sorry. I misjudged you, and we could have been friends."

"It's not too late, you know." Sawyer pulled the yearbook from her hands and closed it. "We're friends now."

"Yes, that's true. But if I could go back…"

"No one gets to go back, Kelsey. We are who we are because of our pasts, and I wouldn't change a single thing about you."

Maybe his parents' attic was an odd place to finally put a name to the feelings he'd started to develop for Kelsey, but as he met her eyes, certainty settled on his heart. It was more than just admiration for her investigative skills, the way he admired how she stayed tough and persevered. There were so many things he liked and appreciated about her. High on the list was the way he couldn't quite seem to get wanting to kiss her out of his mind.

And as he looked at her now, moved slightly closer, he wasn't sure she wasn't thinking of that, too.

His gaze went to her lips.

She lifted her chin.

And then he wrapped her in his arms and kissed her, long and slow, like the past didn't matter and the future stretched before them with all sorts of possibilities.

The kiss ended unhurriedly. As he pulled away, he looked into Kelsey's eyes.

"You kissed me," she said.

"I did."

"But we…"

"What?"

"We can't…"

He picked up one of her hands and held it. "We're adults, Kelsey. We're past all of that stuff from high school, we're not our parents, we're not that different. Any more arguments?"

"My job."

"We can work it out later. But we're a good team, Kelsey. Whatever that looks like, I think it's worth figuring out how to make it work."

Kelsey took a deep breath. "For today, let's focus on the case. One thing at a time, okay?"

It sounded like a brush-off, but the way she smiled at him as she said it softened the words. She felt it, too, she knew that that kiss was more than just a regular kiss. It was the start of something. Even if right now it felt like part of her was still pushing him away.

"Okay. Today, the case." Sawyer put the yearbook box back, pulled out another. "Maybe it's this one." He worked on catching his breath.

"*A Picture History of Treasure Point.* Yes, this one is it."

"Ooh, I've heard of that book but haven't seen it. May I?" Kelsey reached out a hand eagerly, looking like a kid in a candy store. While Sawyer could see what a good law enforcement officer she'd been in the way she worked this case and tackled it head-on, he could also see how she was good with antiques, the way she valued history.

She flipped through the pages. "This is amazing. It talks about the first families here. The Hamiltons were here before anyone. Decades before, although this doesn't explain where they came from. After that were some more families who came over with Oglethorpe, or on other similar expeditions not long after."

"Any other families whose names we know?"

"Ellis, Burton, Burns, Smith, Daniel…"

"None that I recognize."

"Me, neither." Kelsey kept flipping through the book. "This is really interesting stuff, even if it doesn't have much to do with our case. I'd love to borrow it sometime."

"Of course."

She set it down and picked up the next book. *"Debtors Down South."* She raised her eyebrows. "Creative title. And this one is not old." She laughed at the overdone cover with eighties' graphics.

"Yeah, I think that one was done by a cousin somewhere along the line who fancied himself a historian. Clearly he might have been a bit overly ambitious."

"Hey, there could be good stuff in here." She picked it up and began to flip through it. "It talks about how the state was settled largely by debtors and criminals. Some of them were good people and just needed a fresh start, but it says that some turned to piracy."

"Well, the coast provided for it, and it was already a rough area, pirate-wise." He wasn't the history buff that Kelsey was, but even he knew that about the area.

"True."

She set that book down with another small laugh. "You have to give the guy credit for making an effort."

"If you say so."

There was one book with just Hamilton family history. Flipping through that made Sawyer a little more thankful for his family heritage. Mostly the Hamiltons had been hardworking people who took their position in the town seriously but who treated others well. It was really only his parents who had turned their reputation into something it never should have become—more of a status symbol than an obligation to take care of the town well.

The last book in that box was *Pirates of Georgia*. Sawyer opened that up, read the first page and then the second.

"You look like you're into that book. Which one is it?" Kelsey scooted closer, looked over his shoulder. "Oh, nice. Does it say anything about any wrecks that went down in the area the map detailed?"

"I'm not sure yet." But it did seem like it might provide a good link. "It mentions *The Determination*. Also a few other ships. *The Starflight* and *The Fortune*."

Kelsey laughed at the last name. "Really?"

"This mentions one of those families you said earlier. The Burns family?"

"Right. I remember that name."

"Well, apparently they're one of those families who didn't exactly turn into model citizens when they arrived in the Georgia colony."

"Pirates?"

"Yes. Much later than Blackbeard, toward the late 1700s. It appears that half of the family settled down nicely and the other half took to piracy and formed their own terrifying circle in the vacuum of power left after Blackbeard and some other prominent pirates died."

"Burns. Burns…"

Kelsey picked up the history of Treasure Point book again. "Here are the names. Andrew Burns, Ezekiel

Burns, Sarah Burns, Hannah Burns. So which ones of them were pirates?"

"Ezekiel and Hannah."

"Husband and wife?"

He shook his head. "Siblings."

"Interesting! So…where does this fit?"

"I don't know, but it seems like it would fit somewhere. They're tied to at least three shipwrecks that sunk in the approximate area the map detailed."

"Their ships?"

Sawyer read a little further. "One was theirs. Another was one they took over, but it sank soon after. And another they sank themselves after they got the treasure out of it."

"They were *pirate* pirates. They profited off other profiteers."

"It looks like it."

"So they're connected to the wrecks." Kelsey stood and began to pace the attic. "But how does this fit with what we already know? We have a motive for the murder, which we assume was to cover up someone stealing from shipwrecks and selling it."

"And that seems to be supported by what your assistant told you."

Kelsey continued. "That ship has been underwater for over three hundred years. Nothing from the wreck could have ended up on the market if someone hadn't stolen it."

"Not even if the pirates sold it themselves hundreds of years ago?"

"It's a stretch. Their navigational tools? Though they were valuable, they were also tools. They wouldn't have gotten rid of useful tools when they still had the ship. And anyway, if the tools had been sold years ago, there would be records for them dating back through the centuries. This navigational tool only popped up recently." Kelsey was thankful for her history classes, for the foundation she had to understand how some of this would have worked. Who would have thought it would ever tie into an investigation she was working on?

"We also have an old Treasure Point family who was connected to piracy," Kelsey continued.

"Right, but we don't know how that ties in," Sawyer pointed out. "We need to find a link for that. The library? The cemetery?" Sawyer tossed up every idea he had. "Where else would have old records?"

They both went silent. Kelsey shook her head. "I need to eat something, I'm sorry. I can't focus when I'm hungry and I haven't had anything since breakfast."

Sawyer's stomach chose that moment to growl. "Me, neither." They'd both forgotten about lunch amidst the scuba diving aftermath, and then bringing the truck to Shiloh.

"Want to head to town?"

"Let's just get something from downstairs and eat it up here."

"I don't want to face your parents again."

Sawyer couldn't argue with that.

"All right, you stay up here. I'll be right back. Are sandwiches okay?"

"Sounds great." Kelsey smiled at him and Sawyer headed for the stairs.

"And Sawyer?"

He stopped.

"Even though I meant what I said, and we have to focus on the case right now...about earlier?"

He waited.

"I'm not sorry."

FIFTEEN

Kelsey hadn't counted on how empty the attic would feel when Sawyer had left. Empty and kind of creepy. But she was a big girl, not someone who was used to running every time she had a hint of nervousness try to overtake her, so she stayed where she was and reached for another box. Sawyer hadn't said how many contained books like the one they'd already looked through, but it wouldn't hurt to check.

She'd just opened the box lid when the steady hum of the power went silent and the room went dark.

It was too much like the museum, eerily like it. Except she was in the Hamiltons' house right now. No one would dare try to get past their security, right?

But how easy would it have been to follow them there?

No. The power was a coincidence. It had to be. She hoped it was.

Chills crept down slowly, over her shoulders, down her arms. She started to turn around.

And arms grabbed her from behind, pinning her arms to her sides.

"No! Sawyer, help!" Kelsey managed to yell the words at full volume before whoever had her slid something over her head.

A pillowcase?

Her attacker forced her onto the ground, pushed her shoulders so hard into the floor that Kelsey couldn't move her arms at all. She kept kicking and finally connected with something.

Her attacker cried out.

That voice. She'd heard it before. Kelsey couldn't place it now, but it brought to mind crime scenes, high-speed chases.

Her police days. Those were years ago. Was it someone from a past case? No, this had to be connected to the museum, it wasn't just about some felon getting revenge on her. Someone from the department? They had wondered if one of the officers might be covering for the criminal, but until now she hadn't allowed herself to entertain the thought that it might be an officer responsible for everything.

Whoever it was, he forced a pillow over her face. Suffocation? Why didn't he just shoot her and get it over with?

Oh… Kelsey was suddenly grateful they were at Sawyer's parents' house. The Hamiltons were too powerful to risk shooting one of them through the floor. Whichever one was left alive would stop at nothing to find the killer. Whoever had her, he'd thought this through, chosen his method of killing her thoughtfully. Smart. And sick.

He pushed the pillow down harder until Kelsey struggled to draw in a breath. Cotton fabric was all she was breathing, no matter how much she struggled for oxygen.

God, I'm not ready to die. There are things I'd do differently.

It was the same feeling she'd had scuba diving. This desperate need for air.

Come on, Sawyer.

Sawyer. If I had another chance, I wouldn't push him away. I'd kiss him again.

But he wasn't coming. Not fast enough. Kelsey's mind felt sluggish.

I might even have gone back to being a police officer, doing my best to help get people like this behind bars. I feel most alive when I'm doing this, and ironically, it's going to be how I die.

Kelsey continued to struggle, tried to kick her attacker again, but he'd positioned himself so that was impossible. There was no fighting her way out of his, he was too strong. And he wasn't going to stop until she was dead.

Or until he thought she was...

Kelsey went limp.

And heard footsteps on the stairs. Maybe Sawyer would come in time and her attacker wouldn't have the chance to confirm that she was dead.

Yes. As she'd hoped, he'd heard the footsteps, too, and as he got up, the pressure on her released. Did she chase him? Though she had a gun, she didn't want to use it in the house either, not knowing where Sawyer and his parents were. No, they'd catch this guy, find enough evidence to put him away. She didn't need to take it into her own hands right now.

She had to stay still. Kelsey listened as he escaped, kept racking her brain for the voice she'd heard. She knew that voice was someone she knew, someone in Treasure Point, hiding in plain sight among innocent townspeople as they searched everywhere for a killer...

The door creaked open. "I'm back."

Sawyer. Kelsey moved the pillow off her head, slid the pillowcase off her face.

He met her eyes, dropped the food and ran to her.

"What happened? I never thought... I shouldn't have left you!"

"I'm okay," Kelsey said, realizing as she sat up that it was basically true. She rubbed her left shoulder—most of the pressure had been there and she'd likely have a bruise tomorrow, but it was the best that things could have turned out. "He tried to suffocate me, and I pretended to go limp so that he'd think I was dead. I don't know if it would have worked, but he heard your footsteps so he had to hurry out or have two of us to deal with."

"He keeps getting closer." Sawyer's jaw was tighter than she'd ever seen it.

"But so do we," Kelsey countered.

"We need to call the police."

"Not the regular number."

"Why?"

Kelsey shook her head. "I kicked my attacker and he cried out. I can't place it yet, but I know I've heard that voice before, maybe at the police department?"

Sawyer sobered. "I know y'all were starting to suspect that someone was leaking information. But this is different."

Kelsey nodded. "Very different. And I'm not sure yet, so I don't want to say anything to anyone. I just want people I trust looking into this."

"I've got Clay's number in my phone." Sawyer called and told him what had happened. "They're on their way."

The officers didn't take long to arrive. Kelsey told her story, and after Sawyer and Kelsey led them up to the attic to search for evidence, Sawyer grabbed Kelsey's hand and pulled her toward the stairs. "We're going to go get food."

"What?" Was he serious?

"You've got to eat, Kelsey. You're not on the force and there's no reason you need to be up here right now."

She wanted to fight him, but as hungry as she'd been before the attack, she was feeling weaker now. Instead, she nodded. "Okay." And she let him lead her down the stairs.

"I know they'll fill you in anyway, Kels. I'm not trying to keep you out of the loop."

"I know. You're right."

Kelsey sat down on a stool in the kitchen and watched Sawyer fix them lunch again, since the other was spilled all over the attic floor. Sandwiches and chips, perfect.

"Thank you," she said, as he handed her the plate.

"No problem. Sandwiches are easy."

"I mean, for everything. It's not lost on me that I couldn't have done this without you."

He smiled. "Sure you could have."

"But I wouldn't want to try. We're a good team."

They finished eating and went back upstairs.

Clay shook his head when they came in. "The only thing we found was where he got in. There's an access panel back here that leads to the garage. It wouldn't be hard to get in there if someone knew where it was."

"Only the security company does."

"We'll follow up that lead," Clay said. "You two lay low." He looked at Kelsey specifically.

She shook her head. "We have some leads to follow, too."

"Want to share?"

"Not yet. Later, if they turn up anything."

Kelsey grabbed the books they'd been looking at and started for the stairs. "Are you coming?" she asked Sawyer.

He followed her. Kelsey was glad. Brave as she'd been in many situations in her lifetime, the place they needed to go next was not only creepy but very isolated, somewhere she didn't want to set foot in alone.

They killed time at her apartment until dinner, when Kelsey had fixed them spaghetti.

"You're sure about this plan?" Sawyer asked her as he finished up his second helping.

"It's all I can think to do. We need a link between those names and someone, anyone. We need a lead." She hit the table with a balled-up fist. "I'm sick of him coming after me, sick of almost dying. I don't want to live like this."

"I understand. I want this to be over, too. But this feels…"

"Like there are a hundred ways it could go wrong?"

"Exactly."

"If you have a better plan…"

But he didn't, and she knew it. They'd stopped by the library on the way home from his parents' house to see if it was possible they had records dating that far back, but hadn't been able to find anything promising. Treasure Point hadn't fully embraced its history until recently, so many records just hadn't been viewed as important enough to archive, though Sawyer suspected they existed in an attic building or storage building somewhere.

With that option taken from them, going to the cemetery made sense. It did. But it wasn't somewhere that people wandered around regularly, not like some of the hauntingly beautiful graveyards in Savannah that were tourist attractions. This one was just as historical, but not quite as well kept as those. It was closed to new graves—anyone who'd died since 1949 had been buried in a new cemetery closer to Brunswick. Sawyer would rather not go tonight, but it made sense. Every minute they lost was another minute Kelsey was in danger. If they could finish this fast, that was what he wanted.

"It's almost eight. No matter when we leave now it's going to be dark. Sure you don't want to wait until morning?" Sawyer asked.

"No. I don't want to waste any time."

Sawyer nodded. Exactly how he'd felt. "Let's leave around eleven, then. If it's going to be dark anyway, we may as well wait till the middle of the night and reduce the chances of anyone following us. You should try to get some sleep before then," Sawyer suggested. He noticed the way she flinched, and wanted to smack himself on the forehead when he realized that resting her head on a pillow probably sounded terrifying to her right now.

"I don't think so," she said.

"On the couch, come on. I'll sit here." Sawyer settled himself in a chair right beside the couch. "And you can nap right here. If I hear anything, I'll wake you up."

"No, but thanks."

"Listen, Kelsey, I know you're going to have nightmares. But I also know that you won't even try to sleep later tonight. You have to take care of yourself. Please?"

Sawyer watched her face soften a little as some of the fight left it.

"I'll try."

Not ten minutes later Sawyer was watching her sleep.

He was thankful she was able to get a little rest. After what had happened earlier, she needed it.

Speaking of earlier, Sawyer didn't like to think about that. Had he been foolish to leave her alone in the attic while he'd gotten lunch ready? He wouldn't have thought so, still didn't *really* think so, if he were honest. That attack felt like a freak coincidence. But like Kelsey had said, she was probably spared from being shot by the fact that she'd been in his parents' attic, with him and his mother also in the house. Here was another time in the same case that it seemed being a Hamilton was coming in handy.

He disliked the way the name had kept him from friendships like the one he could have had with Kelsey. On the other hand, it had helped them in this case.

He resented the family obligation to continue in the business field, but…was it possible that the family's name and connections could help him create his own job in marine biology? He hadn't heard back about any of his applications, which he suspected was his fault for not putting enough passion into them, because none of the jobs was exactly what he'd wanted. But he had business skills when he took things slow, didn't try to show off like he had that last time. Couldn't he combine those with his marine biology knowledge and come up with a combination that would give him something meaningful to do every day?

He thought about it for a little while, until Kelsey started to stir. Sawyer glanced at his watch. Almost eleven. It had been that long?

"Wake up, Kelsey." He put a hand on her arm, bracing himself in case he got kicked after the traumatizing day she'd had, but she opened her eyes immediately and without panicking.

"Is it time?"

"Yep."

"Let's go."

Sawyer opened the door first, checked for anything out of the ordinary. It was quiet outside. Kelsey came up behind him and they walked to his truck.

The Treasure Point Cemetery was near the ruins of the old lighthouse, but farther from the coast and deeper in the woods. There was no road to the cemetery, not that a car could go down. There was only a path wide enough for people to walk. Some of the original settlements in Treasure Point had been close to this spot, but not long after the town had been settled and the cemetery had been built the town moved up the coast a little. Now this area had been mostly abandoned.

Sawyer parked the truck, turned off the lights. Before he could even unbuckle, Kelsey was out of the truck.

Sawyer hurried after her. "Wait for me, would you?" he whispered as he jogged up behind her on the path.

"Sorry. I just want to figure this out and get back."

"You just can't wait to get yourself in more danger, can you?"

"You think we're walking into something?"

"No." Sawyer had no reason to think that. "But I think anytime we're out in the open, especially in the woods where it would be easy for someone to sneak up on us, there's a risk there that's hard to contain."

"Well, unfortunately we can't solve this case from the apartment I'm staying in, so I'm just going to have to take my chances."

She did have a good point.

"At least slow down. And stay with me." Sawyer reached for her hand and she let him take it. Nice as it felt to have her hand in his, tonight he was being practical. There was a little moonlight, but they were walking deeper and deeper into a pine forest right now and the light was being choked out by the tall trees. He didn't want them to be separated in the dark.

A loud noise in the bushes startled him and he jerked Kelsey backward a little. The noise continued. Kelsey reached in her pocket for a flashlight, shone it on the source of the noise.

"Armadillo." She clicked the light off. "Not the most quiet creatures."

They continued walking down the path, careful to walk slowly and shuffle their feet a little so they didn't trip over any roots. Sawyer was just hoping that there were no snakes on the path, because if there were, they'd never see them.

So far so good on that front, but there were spider webs that kept tangling around them. Some of the orb weavers around here were larger than half-dollars. Sawyer wasn't bothered by spiders, but he didn't particularly want one of those crawling up him to his face, either.

Finally the moonlight grew brighter as they approached a large clearing. The grass was tall, almost to their waists, and Sawyer stopped walking.

"What?"

"Snakes." Sawyer turned his own flashlight on, searched the ground for a stick he could use to sweep the ground in front of them for unwelcome reptiles.

"Good thinking," Kelsey whispered. Sawyer turned his light off.

They moved through the field slowly. The cemetery was at the back edge of it, surrounded by a wrought iron fence. Sawyer had only been here twice. Once on a field trip to learn about Treasure Point's history in elementary school, and once in the middle of the night on an obligatory high school dare, which his parents had been furious about once word had gotten to them. He'd gotten a long talking-to about respecting history, the dead and cemeteries in general, and told that he'd lose his new car—a present for his sixteenth birthday— if he did anything like that again.

Sawyer hadn't been back since.

The fence was coming into view now. They moved closer to it. "So, we get in, try to find those four names to see who they are connected to by marriage, then get out. Right?"

"Right," Kelsey agreed in a hushed voice. "This place gives me the creeps."

"I only came here twice when I was younger."

"I came more than that," Kelsey admitted. "It was history. It kind of fascinated me."

"You really do love history, don't you?" He squeezed her hand without thinking.

"I do." She squeezed back. Smiled. Then looked away.

Together, they moved toward the fence. This was part of what made Sawyer dislike this place—the wrought iron fence was four feet high and there was only one gate. If someone attacked them while they were inside, it wouldn't be easy for them to escape. Thankfully no one should know they were here. He'd taken extra care to make sure they weren't followed—there hadn't even been cars close to where they were on the roads tonight. Sawyer wasn't taking chances with Kelsey's safety.

Kelsey let go of his hand and reached for the gate. It squeaked as she opened it, protesting years of disrepair and neglect. It was a shame that no one was looking after this place. Sawyer should come out here in the daytime with some WD-40. He would, as soon as this was all over and life returned to seminormal.

She walked through the gate first, through the tall grass, although it was slightly shorter in here. The first gravestones weren't far away. Picking their way through the aisles—that lecture about respect his parents had given him years ago had really stuck—they moved around quietly, each of them reading the stones in silence.

Rebecca Hall Wallace. Harrison Wallace. Not names he'd heard of.

Rich Smith. Samantha Smith. Also not the ones they were looking for.

Finally there was a name he recognized from the books. Andrew Burns. Sarah Burns. Buried side by side. "The two of them must have been married."

"Where are the other Burnses? The ones who were pirates? They're the ones we need to find."

Ezekiel Burns.

"He never married."

"Well that's a dead end." Kelsey winced. "No pun intended."

They wandered the aisles a little longer. Sawyer was beginning to worry that the other Burns, Hannah, had died somewhere else and not been buried here. If that was the case, he didn't know where they'd resume their search, how they'd go about finding a link between the shipwrecks and anyone in town.

"There," Kelsey whispered. She stopped. Turned to Sawyer, her eyes wide with disbelief.

Jacob Davies. *Hannah Burns Davies.*

"Lieutenant Davies."

"That's… Yes," Kelsey said. "Now that I have the name, it was his voice I heard in the attic. So then… he's the one—" he watched her swallow hard "—who is trying to kill me."

SIXTEEN

"We need to tell someone," Sawyer stated the obvious and Kelsey nodded.

"Let's go."

They crept back across the cemetery without incident and were almost through the gate when the first gunshot hit the ground inches from her feet, kicking up dirt and bits of grass.

"Get down." Sawyer's voice wasn't loud, but it was firm.

"No, run!"

She felt him hesitating beside her, but Kelsey took off anyway, dodging bullets as she ran. Finally Sawyer caught up.

They had to stop to open the gate, and that's when fire flew through Kelsey's arm. She yelled.

"You're hit!" Sawyer grabbed her other arm, pulled her off into the woods. "Get down," he said in a softer voice this time, presumably so their shooter wouldn't hear.

Kelsey got on her knees, but when she tried to put weight on her hand to crawl, the fire exploded in her arm again and she couldn't move. She bit back tears, hopelessness falling like a dark cloud she couldn't shrug off.

"I can't move, Sawyer. My arm hurts too bad." She hated feeling helpless like this. While she had her gun in her holster and could shoot with her off hand, it would be foolish and irresponsible to shoot at an unseen target.

"You have to. There's a dry creek bed this way. It's not far, but hopefully Davies doesn't know it's here. Not everybody who grew up here does."

Kelsey hadn't known about it, so she could only hope that he was right and Davies didn't, either. She did her best to follow him, putting most of her weight on her legs and left arm. When she had to use her right, she gritted her teeth and tried to be thankful it was her arm that had gotten hit and not anything more vital. Kelsey still couldn't believe she'd spent a short career as a police officer without incident, but couldn't manage to work as an antiques insurance agent without getting injured and attacked multiple times.

The shooting had stopped. Did that mean Davies was creeping closer, lining up another shot? Kelsey hoped not, and felt like the darkness in this part of the woods was on their side. He wouldn't be able to see as well here, away from the light of the moon.

"There's a spot just up ahead…" Sawyer trailed off. "It's not far. Hang in there, Kels."

She followed him ten more yards until he stopped at a fallen tree that overhung the creek bed. Brambles and branches had grown up around it to provide a little bit of shelter. It was perfect for hiding.

"You crawl in first. I'll stay on the outside, just in case he does come back."

"It's not even your case. I dragged you into this. You shouldn't be in the line of fire." Her words came out choppily as she tried to speak past the pain.

"Just let me take care of you, okay? I know you can handle yourself, but maybe I want to help."

She didn't have anything to say to that. Her parents had raised her to be self-sufficient, maybe to a fault. But ever since she'd run into Sawyer at the museum party he'd been going out of his way to show her that she didn't have to do everything all on her own. But like he'd just said, he'd never acted like she was incapable in any way. He just wanted to help.

Kelsey squeezed her eyes at the tears that were building. She didn't know for sure if they were because of the bullet hole in her arm, the fact that spiders were probably crawling all over her—the one creature she couldn't stand—or the realization that Sawyer was so much more than the cocky, overconfident kid he'd been in high school. He'd grown into a man who was sure enough of himself to let her handle her own rescues, but who was there to help her if she needed it.

He was turning very much into the sort of man she could see herself falling in love with. But there was still the matter of her job, and his. He couldn't study ocean life traveling from place to place around Georgia.

But then again, traveling around was starting to lose its appeal for Kelsey, too. She remembered her thoughts up in the attic, when she'd thought she was about to die. In those moments, she'd regretted giving up police work, which had always made her feel invigorated and alive, confident in the knowledge that she was making a difference.

But could she really give up the dream she'd planned on, worked so hard for?

"I'm going to text the chief," Sawyer said in a low voice. Kelsey looked at her arm while he did so. There was blood, but not as much as she'd expected. As much as it hurt, it looked like the bullet had just grazed the outside of her arm, which was painful, but not as bad as a through-and-through shot would have been.

"Oh, no."

Kelsey sat up a little, senses on alert, at Sawyer's tone. "What's wrong?"

"The chief says he's already heard about the shots being fired. He says Davies is in the area and is supposed to see about it."

"No. Text him back."

"I am."

Kelsey made herself take deep breaths, knowing how easy it would be to work herself up into a state where she wouldn't do much good. She needed to stay calm; it was just easier said than done. Much easier.

"I can't imagine what he's told them," she muttered. They had contacted the police as soon as they could, but Davies obviously had an advantage since he'd planned this attack. What they needed to do was get control back. But how?

Sawyer's voice broke into her thoughts. "I'm going to tell the chief our location, so he can tell Davies."

"Have you lost your mind?"

"And then we're going to loop around the cemetery, behind it, but close enough to know when Davies heads this way that there's no chance he'll be able to surprise us. We should be able to hear him the whole time, breaking through the trees."

"Not to be a party pooper, Sawyer, but doesn't that mean he'll hear us, too?"

"We're going to keep walking up this creek bed."

"This is the only dry spot." Kelsey continued arguing. Did she not *want* a plan to get out of this alive?

"So we'll wade through the creek. It's not very deep, and it's the only sure way to not make noise."

"And what if he decides to go through the creek, too? We'll walk right into him."

"No, he won't do that when there's a game trail directly here from the cemetery. That's what we took. Why did you think it was so easy to run here when the woods in Georgia are thick with thorns and everything else?"

"I didn't think about it. But it does make sense." She gave him a small smile. "You're better at this than I thought."

"That was almost a compliment, thanks. Now, let's go."

Sawyer reached down and helped her up. Wincing a little as it jarred her hurt shoulder, Kelsey stood up.

"You need a doctor."

"I don't think I'm going to argue with you about that."

"There's a first time for everything." He smiled to lighten her mood a little. Her energy and determination were starting to fade, ever so slightly, probably from the shock of everything. At least it was reassuring that she really was human and not the unstoppable, unflappable dynamo she seemed to be. This was the first sign of weakness she'd shown, and they couldn't afford for her to settle into that discouragement, not now when their safety depended on moving fast and believing this would work.

The dry creek bed soon turned to damp mud, which let them walk a little faster since there were no leaves to crunch loudly. Soon the creek was back to its normal depth, six inches or so, and they slogged through it, not adding any more noise to the slight rushing the creek already made.

"How far are we?"

"Not far."

They walked for another few minutes, then Sawyer reached out and grabbed Kelsey's uninjured arm. "Stop," he mouthed and held up a hand. He pointed through the trees, to where he could see someone walking. It could be Davies—the height and build were right—but he was dressed in a gillie suit, a camouflage outfit that made it impossible to see someone unless they were moving. Sawyer was grateful that his message had gotten passed from the chief to Davies, and even more thankful that his plan seemed to be working and Davies had done what Sawyer had anticipated.

They really should be able to do this.

Five more minutes of creek walking and they were behind the cemetery. This was the most dangerous part. Their would-be killer could easily have backtracked.

There was no way to tell.

"This is the risky part," he whispered.

"Yep."

As noiselessly as possible, they climbed out of the creek and crept toward the cemetery. Being surrounded by physical reminders of death when someone wanted you dead was a sobering thing.

No sign of danger.

They made it through the field and Sawyer exhaled as they stepped into the cover of the woods. They moved along the path, each step taking them closer to help.

The gunshots started again. Davies must have heard them somehow.

This time neither of them shouted. They just both took off at a sprint, Kelsey a little slower than she had been earlier, due to her arm. Still, somehow they made it to the place where they'd parked without any further injuries. In one motion, Sawyer unlocked the doors and reached for Kelsey. "Get in!" He helped her into the driver's seat and she scooted over to the passenger side to make room for him.

Sawyer got inside without incident, slammed the door and hit the gas, relieved when the engine immediately roared to life. First, he'd get Kelsey to the hospital to get that graze taken care of. Next, he'd be stopping by the Treasure Point Police Department. Surely if he talked to them in person, someone would believe what they'd discovered tonight.

Sawyer hadn't expected to be face-to-face with Lieutenant Davies at the police station less than an hour after the man had tried to kill both him and Kelsey. At least Kelsey wasn't here yet, although she'd made no secret of the fact that she planned to come right over after she was finished at the hospital. Sawyer had decided it was safe enough there with so many doctors, but just in case, he'd asked a friend of his who worked at the hospital to keep an extra close eye on her until she left, without explaining why.

When Kelsey did get here, it wasn't going to be pretty—Sawyer was fairly certain she wouldn't be able to hold in the anger she felt toward the man for wreaking so much havoc on her life.

In fact, Sawyer wasn't sure how he was going to hold it in, either.

He took a deep breath, put on his best business face and told himself to play it cool.

"Lieutenant Davies."

"Sawyer." The other man nodded and continued walking down the hall.

Doubt shook Sawyer. They were right, weren't they? The evidence they had pointing to Davies was all circumstantial, yes. But he trusted Kelsey when she said she'd recognized his voice. The chief would believe her, too…wouldn't he?

Clay Hitchcock walked into the station just then. "Sawyer. I heard about the shots fired. Everyone okay?"

"Kelsey's getting checked out at the hospital. A bullet grazed her."

"I'm glad it wasn't worse."

"Listen, I've got to talk to you. Is there anywhere…" Sawyer looked around the open area where they were standing. "Anywhere else we can talk?"

"Sure." Clay led him to one of the rooms off the hallway, let him inside.

"What is it?"

"We think Davies was the guy shooting at us," Sawyer said in a low voice.

"Not possible." Clay shook his head. "I know we've been on edge here, and I still think there's a leak, but I don't think it's one of our officers, especially not one with that much seniority."

"Kelsey says…"

"Kelsey has a grudge against Davies. Did she tell you about why she left here?"

"I thought you were one of the ones who believed in her."

Clay exhaled. "I do. But even the best cop can get on the wrong track because of whatever biases he or she brings to the case."

Sawyer didn't know what to say to that, how to proceed. What would Kelsey want him to do? Should he share the information they'd found out, or keep it to himself for now? She'd probably tell him to quit talking, to get out of there.

That was what he'd decided to do, but Hitchcock kept talking.

"You are right that he is connected. He came to us before you got here, and confessed that he's been covering for someone, though he insists he didn't leak any information. He wouldn't tell us who he was covering for, said he didn't want to get in any deeper than he already was. He was supposed to meet the guy at an old dock on the Hamilton property at dawn."

"And you're going to go?"

Hitchcock was nodding. "I came in early to get a plan together. We're all meeting now, so I've got to go."

"All right."

He opened the door and started to walk away.

"Sawyer! Clay!" Kelsey burst through the front doors, arm bandaged, but besides that not showing any signs of having been hurt. "Wait!"

She hurried to them.

"I already told him, Kelsey," Sawyer said in a low voice once she was close enough that no one would overhear their conversation.

"You did? So did you arrest him?" She looked at Clay.

Clay's expression was like the clouds before the storm, a warning of what was coming. Sawyer braced himself.

Kelsey was not going to like this.

"We have no reason to believe there's a need for that."

"What?" Kelsey couldn't keep the disbelief out of her tone.

"We've never had any cause to think one of our own was behind the murders themselves, even if we have suspected a leak or something to that effect." Clay said the words calmly, but the calm didn't rub off on Kelsey. She felt anything but.

"What if we've been wrong?" Kelsey looked straight at Clay, feeling confident in herself and her instincts in a way she hadn't in years. Without thinking, she was the old Kelsey again, but more self-assured. Ready to be who she was.

Which was apparently law enforcement, through and through.

"We appreciate your help, Kelsey. And when you were an officer, no one respected the job you did more than me, okay? But we can't afford to be wrong here. Sawyer already told me what you're thinking. You're implying…"

"I'm not implying. I'm saying. Lieutenant Davies is behind everything."

"There's no reason to think that besides circumstantial evidence, Kelsey. And it's inadmissible in court for a reason—because it's not reliable."

"But I am. I heard his voice when he attacked me in the attic. It was definitely Davies."

"You are reliable, but you're also a human. Look, it's nothing personal. We're family, okay? I trusted you through that whole Hamilton robbery debacle years ago. But this is different."

"It's not."

"It is. And besides, Lieutenant Davies has confessed to covering up for a guy. That's huge, Kelsey, and not something he would do if it wasn't true. So you're partly right, I guess. You probably pegged the leak in the department, even though he's still claiming at this point that he didn't share any information. As surprising as that is, it wasn't a malicious thing. Just a lapse in judgment."

"There is *no* guy he's helping, or that he's covering up for. It's him, it's always been him and this is some kind of setup."

Clay was already shaking his head, the look of trust that was always on his face now replaced by something Kelsey was far more used to seeing…hesitation. "You have no proof."

"Not yet, but we'll get it. We can't bring him in without it, but we'll have it. Just believe me." Kelsey was sick of this. She was willing to put herself in Davies's crosshairs one last time if it would prove that he was the one after her, if it would result in him being locked up and no longer free to terrorize her.

"I can't help you, Kelsey. I can't take that kind of chance. He's a fellow officer, a good officer with decades of honorable service, and I think maybe you're just so desperate for this to be over that you're seeing connections where there aren't any."

She looked to Sawyer. "What do you think?"

Clay followed her gaze. They both waited.

"I believe you." Sawyer didn't even hesitate.

Kelsey smiled.

"Hitchcock! It's time to go!" O'Dell stuck his head out of one of the rooms and yelled down the hallway of the police station.

"You heard him. We've got a planning meeting and then the meet. Hopefully the guy stays ignorant of the fact that it's a setup and no one gets hurt, us or Davies or the killer. Once we bring him in, we can finally get some answers."

"I'm telling you, there is no other man."

"I'm not going to start suspecting the men and women I work with of murder, Kelsey. There's enough anti-officer sentiment in the country without other police-men adding to it."

"I'm right, Clay. I can feel it." Couldn't she? She wanted to second-guess herself, to fade back into the shadows of her other job, get out of this investigation, but she couldn't. This was who she was. And she was sure.

Clay shook his head. "Be careful, Kelsey. Whoever is after you is still out there. Don't let your theory keep you from protecting yourself from whoever might be after you."

Clay walked down the hallway to the room where the other officers were waiting to start their meeting. Kelsey glanced at Sawyer, crept closer to the room and stood there just long enough to hear the location Davies had suggested they meet with "the suspect" he'd theo-retically been covering for.

Only there was no other man. Kelsey was sure, deep inside.

She hurried back down the hall to Sawyer. They exited the police station and walked across the parking lot, head-ing straight for Sawyer's truck.

"We've got to meet them there." Kelsey reached for the passenger door of the truck.

Sawyer opened his own door and climbed in as she did. "Are you sure that's a good idea? Clay didn't seem very happy with your theory—he might get upset if we show up."

"It's not me he's upset with, it's the idea of a police-man breaking the law. He doesn't want to believe that it could be true." She shook her head. "Clay is loyal to a fault. It was good when I was the one who needed him to stick by me, not be willing to believe some of the negative things that were said, but this is different."

"I don't know if I hope you're right or hope you're wrong," Sawyer admitted as he put the truck in Drive.

"Let's hope I'm right, so this can be over."

"Where's the meet?"

"Do you know where the old dock on the Hamilton property is?"

"Yep."

"Drive us there."

Sawyer navigated the truck in that direction, but when Kelsey thought he should have been turning left down an old dirt road, he drove straight.

"What are you doing?"

"Sawyer *Hamilton*, remember? I know another way. If you're hoping to walk up in the middle of their meeting and possibly get shot, then sure, let's go back to the way everyone in town knows about. But otherwise I think we have a better chance using this path."

She'd give him that. "Thanks. I didn't know about this way."

"Not many people do. I guess that Hamilton thing does come in handy sometimes."

"You sound as surprised as I am," Kelsey teased.

"So what's the plan?"

"Call the chief. We never were able to talk to him. He's the only one with seniority over Davies. Maybe he will believe us."

She did. "He's not answering." She disconnected the call.

"Call him again, and this time, leave a message. Tell him where we are in case we end up needing backup."

"But we're supposed to be *their* backup."

"I know. But there's no telling how this is going to go down."

"You're right." Kelsey called the chief's number

again. "Chief, this is Kelsey." She paused, talking about Davies was too weird for voice mail. Then again, didn't he need to know? "We're headed to an old dock on the Hamilton property, hopefully to apprehend the killer. Sir... I've got to be honest, Clay disagrees with me, and O'Dell probably does, too, but I firmly believe that the killer is a Treasure Point police officer. I believe it's Lieutenant Davies. I'll check in with you in an hour. If you haven't heard from me by then, please send more backup to the spot where the meet with Davies was supposed to take place. Bye."

SEVENTEEN

A few days ago, Kelsey had listened to an attack that had taken a man's life. Now she was creeping through the woods, watching for any sign of danger, wondering if today would be the day that *she* would die.

"This is a stupid idea. We're walking into a trap. It's not too late to go home," she whispered to Sawyer.

He reached for her hand. Squeezed it once. "The trap isn't meant for us—it's meant for O'Dell and Hitchcock. You don't want to leave them without backup, do you?"

She shuddered at the thought of something happening to her cousin. "No, of course not."

She could see Hitchcock and O'Dell moving toward the abandoned dock, using extreme caution. As far as Kelsey could tell, no one else was there yet, not Davies or the theoretical suspect the officers were expecting to meet there.

That last part didn't surprise her, since Kelsey was sure there *was* no other person. It was Davies. What his plan was remained to be seen, but knowing him, she was sure he had one.

She moved just a little closer, as carefully as she could, to a spot behind an oak tree and some tangled thorn bushes that served as pretty good cover. Sawyer followed and settled in beside her. His presence beside her made her feel stronger, made her feel more like who she really was. That was good, because she needed the confidence right now.

Sawyer reached for her hand, and she looked at him, eyes catching his in a way she hadn't expected. She squeezed back, smiled a little and took a deep breath.

Time to focus.

Kelsey could feel her heartbeat in her chest as they waited. She was hyperaware, felt the tickle of the branches she was leaning against, the slight wind through her hair, the way the air was humid and warm...

Had it really only been days ago that she'd planned to blow into town, do her job as quickly as possible, get the house ready to sell, and then leave and never come back?

Now here she was, lying in the dirt, back doing what she was starting to believe she was meant to do. Years before, when she'd joined the force, she'd convinced herself that police work was just a temporary stop for her along the way to her bigger plans, but had she been wrong?

Kelsey didn't know now. What she did know was that she'd taken list making and goal setting too far. She'd made control her ultimate purpose in life and refused to listen to God if what He said didn't categorize nicely into a box in her mind.

The realization hit her with an almost physical thud in her chest.

God, that's not having a relationship with You. It's... it's worse than treating You like my own personal wish granter. You are the Giver of good things, but they're the good things You choose. Sometimes...

Kelsey swallowed hard.

Sometimes people just can't plan for those. And when

I couldn't plan for them, I just ignored them, tried to pretend like You weren't giving me anything.

It would be so easy to make excuses, to shut off this uncomfortable realization in her mind. But Kelsey didn't want that, she wanted something more this time. *Is that it, God? Do You want me to realize that sometimes when we feel out of control, we see You clearest? I'm sorry. I'll work on giving it up. You be in charge.*

Kelsey felt like her hands were full and empty at the same time. Full of possibilities, of the excitement of knowing that God could do anything with a heart surrendered to him, but empty because she'd used them for so long to hold so tightly to the illusion of control that had been one of the most important things in her life.

And now...

It was gone. Kelsey exhaled.

Movement caught her eye.

"There's Davies. What's the plan?" Sawyer asked.

For once, Kelsey didn't have one. She shook her head. "I have no idea," she whispered as quietly as she could. "Watch, be careful, and if I have to pull my gun, stay back and out of the line of fire."

"Where is he?" O'Dell asked. Kelsey was thankful she'd moved closer so they were within hearing range of the dock, though still far enough back to remain unseen.

"He should be here."

Kelsey watched Davies, analyzed his movements. Surely he wasn't planning to kill both other officers. He couldn't get away with that. At least, Kelsey didn't think so. And what would it accomplish? Getting rid of these men wouldn't stop the investigation, it would just accelerate it. But watching the slow, calculated steps he took, she wasn't sure Davies planned for anyone other than him to walk away alive. Maybe he planned to kill them and frame someone else for their deaths. It was impossible to know for sure, but he seemed to have a plan. Kelsey watched, holding her breath.

Clay moved his hand to his sidearm and Davies drew his faster. "What, did you see something?" Davies asked, still playing the part. Kelsey's muscles were tense. He had to give himself away. O'Dell looked like he didn't know what to think—Kelsey hadn't shared her theory with him—and Clay looked torn up.

He was realizing that she was right. But now there was nothing he could do. To admit that he was onto Davies was to sign his own death warrant, but how long could he play along?

Movement to her left caught her eye and Kelsey glanced that way. Shiloh and the chief. Shiloh put a finger up to her mouth and met Kelsey's eyes. Then she held up a hand, mouthed "Wait."

That's what Kelsey would do. Seemed like something she should have done more in her life, rather than being in such a hurry to make progress on her plans. What had she missed in life so far because of her refusal to wait?

She already knew the answer to that. One of the biggest answers to that question was four inches to her right. If they got out of this unharmed… Kelsey was going to have to think of a way to get him to ask her out on a date.

"I just feel like there's more going on here than it seems," Clay said in a level voice, meeting the lieutenant's eyes the entire time.

Kelsey watched Matt, beside Clay. He also unholstered his weapon slowly, and Kelsey didn't think he knew why, but he trusted his partner's lead. That was how it was supposed to work.

One more moment of calm, of stillness, and then everything exploded, like dry grass with a match tossed in it.

Davies turned, gun still in his hand, and sprinted through the woods away from the dock. Whatever his plan had been, he'd clearly abandoned it now. They finally had the upper hand—now if only they could keep it, they might end this.

The other two officers sprinted after him, and Kelsey stood, looking over at Sawyer. "What do we do?"

He shook his head. "Stand here and stay out of the line of fire."

He was right. This wasn't over yet.

O'Dell tackled Davies and the two men grappled. Kelsey flinched every time she heard another fist connect to someone.

Shiloh and the chief ran in the direction of the scuffle.

Finally, they'd managed to subdue the lieutenant.

Shiloh slid the handcuffs on, smiling a little as she did so. "I never liked you, Davies. And also, you're under arrest."

"What are you doing?" Davies tried to protest. "My contact…"

"Just stop. There is no contact, and we all know it," Kelsey said to him as she walked over to where the officers had things under control. She wasn't going to get in the way, but she had a few things she wanted to say, too.

"How dare you, Davies? You tried to kill me, not just once, but a lot of times. Someone who once worked under your command. We were never close, but I respected you as my superior and a man I thought was a good officer."

"I *am* those things. You're making a mistake."

"I don't think we are," the chief said, then he looked

at Shiloh. "You weren't quite as careful covering your tracks as you thought you were, Davies."

"What are you talking about?" he blustered.

"I have eyewitness testimony that puts you at the dive shop on the morning Kelsey's equipment was tampered with," Shiloh said.

"Circumstantial," Davies said, sneering.

"I also found fingerprints in the dive shop in the one place the owner forgot to clean after you asked him to erase all evidence you were there in return for continuing to ignore some minor criminal infractions going on at the shop. The prints and his testimony should be more than enough."

"And when you can get a warrant for his house, you should find plundered goods and antiques from several shipwrecks near the coast of Treasure Point. I'd say those are pretty solid pieces of evidence," Kelsey added.

Davies had nothing to say to that.

But Kelsey smiled as they hauled him away to the nearest waiting patrol car.

It looked like this was finally over.

Back at the police department, in Treasure Point's only interrogation room, the truth was finally being brought to light. The chief was in the room with Davies—since he was the only one who outranked him and was madder than a rattlesnake that one of his own had committed such crimes.

The rest of them were gathered on the other side of the two-way mirror—a new addition to the station in the last year that was coming in handy right now. Sawyer hadn't seen a police interrogation before.

"You don't understand," Davies whined.

"Don't understand what it's like to kill an innocent man? You're right. I don't understand that."

"It was a victimless crime. No one ever needed to know about it."

"You call second-degree homicide a victimless crime?"

Davies finally flinched. "Before…before that."

The chief wisely said nothing, just let the silence settle into Davies.

"But the museum found out about your shipwreck plundering, and Wingate was going to report you."

Davies dropped his head to his chest. "I've known about those wrecks since I was a kid. My family…"

"The pirate connections. We know."

Davies lifted his head to glare through the glass, presumably at Kelsey.

"I figured I had as good a claim to them as anybody, and I started diving there as a hobby. I was collecting some of the items for myself. I never had any intention of selling them. Until…"

"Until you found out what they were worth, I assume."

Davies sighed. "Yes. So I started selling them. When the museum was set to open soon, I began to wonder if my family's connection to pirate history would be included, and if that could connect me to the things I'd been recovering."

"*Stealing* or *plundering* is more accurate than *recovering.*"

Davies ignored him, continuing his self-justifying rant. "I did some research and found out how harsh the penalties were…so when I was in that room on the night of the opening and Wingate commented on the map and asked me if I'd been to any of those places, and said he'd heard once that my ancestors had been responsible for the wrecks, I decided he knew too much."

"And you killed him."

"I did."

"That may be enough premeditation for first-degree homicide." The chief shook his head. "You were a good cop, Davies. At least, I thought so. Badge." He held out his hand and the lieutenant removed the metal shield from his uniform.

The chief picked up his radio. "I need someone to arrange prisoner transport to the Glynn County Detention Center."

Sawyer recognized that as a prison in Brunswick, not far away.

"Must have decided he was too high risk to go to McIntosh County. It's more of a temporary facility," Kelsey commented under her breath.

The chief had Davies stand and led him out of the room toward the holding area.

Kelsey exhaled beside him. "It's really over."

"It is." They walked together back into the hallway of the police department. The case had taken so much of his thoughts and energy that he hadn't considered much about what would happen now that it was over. "Now I guess you'll go back to Savannah?" He held the door open for her as she walked outside. The chief had asked them to come back later when he was finished overseeing Davies's transport for a more thorough debriefing about the case.

"I...I'm not sure."

Something about the way she looked at him... She'd pushed him away in the attic after that amazing kiss and Sawyer had backed off. But now? She seemed to be inviting the opposite.

"Why don't we walk and talk, and see if we can figure things out."

She nodded, more quiet than he'd ever seen her. "That would be good."

They headed toward the dock.

"I'm going to stay here in town," Sawyer told her. "I've decided to use some of my family's connections to start a marine wildlife research center here in Treasure Point. It's a slightly different ecosystem than Savannah. They're minor variations, but who knows how much impact it could have on what we could learn if there was a center here."

"That sounds amazing. It's just what you've always wanted to do, right? What you've really wanted?"

Sawyer nodded. "It is. I tried living my life my dad's way, and it didn't work. I'm hoping he can come to appreciate the work I'll be doing."

"I hope so."

"What about you?"

Kelsey studied him, still seeming uncertain. "I…I don't know."

"The queen of plans doesn't know hers?" he teased. But Kelsey just shook her head, looking more unsure than he'd ever seen her.

"Well," Sawyer started as he reached for her hand, a motion that had become familiar for the purpose of keeping her close, keeping them both safe during this case, but that meant so much more now. "I think…you've put your dreams on hold long enough. And whatever pursuing those means… I think you should do it."

He couldn't read her expression. He knew they'd come a long way from the way she'd viewed him when she'd first come back to town. Was she finally ready to take this a step further?

Sawyer continued. "But if one of those dreams might happen to be staying here in Treasure Point, whether you continue in the antiques business or go back to law enforcement, I'd really like it if I could be part of it."

This was the part that terrified him.

Sawyer knelt on one knee. "I don't have a ring yet, Kelsey. I have one that's been in my family for years, but I thought maybe, instead of continuing with past traditions, we could take those stones, combine them with others that you'll pick out and create a new setting. Something old, mixed with something new to remind us of the future. If you say yes, I mean."

She laughed a little. "You haven't asked me anything yet."

A grin spread across his face. She was enjoying this. "Kelsey Jackson, I've never met anyone who I felt was such a good match for me, or that I was for them. I love being on a team with you, competing with you, taking care of you and watching you take care of everyone around you. Would you do me the honor of becoming my wife, of marrying me?"

Kelsey laughed again, but this time she also nodded. "Yes, Sawyer, I'd love to be your wife." Another laugh. "Who would have thought I'd fall in love with a Hamilton?"

Sawyer stood and wrapped her in his arms. "And become a Hamilton yourself. When can we get married, Kelsey?"

"As soon as possible," she whispered, and lifted her face to accept his kiss.

EPILOGUE

Kelsey and Sawyer had set a date in September. It wasn't far, just a few months out, but it was more than enough time to plan the low-key wedding the two of them wanted. They were going to hold their reception at the Treasure Point History Museum, which had officially opened without incident only a week before. The wedding ceremony itself would be on the beach.

Sawyer's parents had almost lost it over the beach aspect—Kelsey could still hear his mother's protests about how she was supposed to wear high heels in the sand—but in the end, they'd admitted that it did sound like the sort of thing that would make Sawyer happy and said that that was all they really wanted. Go figure.

Kelsey had accepted a job with the museum as a private security guard—that is, when she wasn't working shifts with the police department. After a lot of thinking and praying, she'd decided that she wasn't ready to give up the antiques world and her degree altogether, but that she loved law enforcement and didn't want to walk away from that, either.

Sawyer was still working on the logistics for his marine wildlife center, but that was keeping him plenty busy.

Their wedding day was cloudless—a huge blessing

in the middle of what was shaping up to be an unusually active hurricane season.

"Almost ready?" Kelsey's mom asked her as the woman doing her makeup applied the finishing touches.

"I think so. Right?"

The other woman nodded. "You're all set." Then she moved aside and Kelsey could see her reflection in the mirror.

"I look…"

"You look beautiful," her mom told her. She pulled her into a hug. "You've always been beautiful. And so strong and independent."

"Thanks, Mom." Kelsey smiled.

"We probably let you be too independent." Her mom hesitated. "Thank you for your willingness to handle the repairs on the house. We never should have left you with such a huge project, but we appreciate the work you did."

Kelsey hugged her mom, feeling tears well up. "Thanks, Mom."

"Careful, don't mess up your makeup," her mom cautioned, but she smiled.

"It's time!" Someone called from the hallway, and Kelsey eased the door open of the portable dressing room that they'd had brought to the beach. She made her way to the back of the aisle.

Sawyer's eyes met hers.

A slow smile spread across her face. It was funny how thoroughly she'd fallen head over heels for a man she'd once thought she had so little in common with.

The music started, but Kelsey barely heard it. She was so lost in her own memories, in the feelings of right now, in the crazy truth that she was about to get married to Sawyer Hamilton.

It was hard to believe they'd been reunited, and had

ended up falling in love. Then again, they weren't the only ones. As Kelsey walked up the aisle slowly, trying to take everything in like her mom had told her to, Kelsey saw Shiloh and Adam Cole, who were expecting their first baby, she'd heard through the grapevine. They'd had a troubled history, back before Shiloh came to town, but they had found their way to love. There was Matt and Gemma O'Dell—a couple with their own high school backstory due to a crime Gemma had witnessed that Matt's father had committed—and their new baby. Claire, Gemma's sister and another friend of Kelsey's from high school, was there with her new husband, Nate. Kelsey didn't know that couple as well, but she'd heard that they'd known each other before, but fallen in love here in town, too.

It was funny, but it made sense at the same time. God certainly worked in surprising ways.

Maybe Treasure Point was just a special place, a place that lent itself to giving people second chances at relationships that they otherwise would have written off. And it had drawn most of those people back to the town, to put down roots where they'd been raised, here in this little corner of South Georgia.

Treasure Point had a way of getting to a person's heart.

It certainly had a place in hers.

* * * * *

Dear Reader,

I can't believe it's time to leave Treasure Point! This fictional town will probably always be special to me, because it was the setting for my debut novel, and I have had a lot of fun with the characters there and the place itself. Thank you for reading my stories and being part of this fictional community with me.

When I was writing Kelsey and Sawyer's story, I realized their spiritual thread was a little less obvious than in some of my other books. It took a while (as it sometimes does in my writing process) to figure out exactly what they were learning and then I realized (as usual) that they were learning what I have been learning lately. Right now, that's the fact that God is not a convenient addition to our day, or an item on a checklist. He is God and He wants to have a relationship with us. That's a huge truth that I don't always live out the way I should, but I am glad I was reminded of it through this story.

I hope that reading this book encouraged you, or entertained you, or both, and I want to thank you again for being a reader, for loving stories. I love doing this job and am grateful for the opportunity to do it—something that couldn't happen without you.

I love hearing from readers, and I'd love to hear from you! You can get in touch with me through email at sarahvarland@gmail.com, find me on Facebook at facebook.com/sarahvarlandauthor, or find me on my personal blog at espressoinalatteworld.blogspot.com.

Sarah Varland

COMING NEXT MONTH FROM
Love Inspired® Suspense

Available March 7, 2017

MISTAKEN IDENTITY
Mission: Rescue • by Shirlee McCoy

When Trinity Miller's attacked by a man who believes she's Mason Gains's girlfriend, the former army pilot turned reclusive prosthetic maker is forced from seclusion to rescue her. But the assailant won't stop targeting her—unless Mason gives up information on one of his clients.

HER BABY'S PROTECTOR
by Margaret Daley and Susan Sleeman

As babies are thrust into danger in two brand-new novellas, these men will stop at nothing to keep them—and their lovely single mothers—safe.

PLAIN SANCTUARY • by Alison Stone

Running her new Amish community bed-and-breakfast, Heather Miller believes she's finally safe from her violent ex-husband—until he escapes from prison to come after her. Now her only hope of survival is relying on US Marshal Zach Walker for protection.

THE SEAL'S SECRET CHILD
Navy SEAL Defenders • by Elisabeth Rees

When former SEAL Edward "Blade" Harding receives an email from his six-year-old son, he's shocked—both by the news that he has a child and by his son's message. Someone's threatening to kill Blade's ex-fiancée, defense attorney Josie Bishop...and she and their little boy need his help.

SECURITY DETAIL
Secret Service Agents • by Lisa Phillips

A mobster is after the former president's daughter Kayla Harris, and she's not sure why. But undercover Secret Service agent Conner Thorne's determined to find out...and save her life.

OUTSIDE THE LAW • by Michelle Karl

Former military recruit Yasmine Browder plans to uncover the truth about her brother's death...but her investigation quickly turns deadly. And her childhood friend rookie FBI agent Noel Black risks his career—and his life—to help her solve the mystery.

_____

LOOK FOR THESE AND OTHER LOVE INSPIRED BOOKS WHEREVER BOOKS ARE SOLD, INCLUDING MOST BOOKSTORES, SUPERMARKETS, DISCOUNT STORES AND DRUGSTORES.

LISCNM0217

SPECIAL EXCERPT FROM

Love Inspired
SUSPENSE

When Trinity Miller's attacked by a man who believes she's Mason Gains's girlfriend, the former army pilot turned reclusive prosthetic maker is forced from seclusion to rescue her. But the assailant won't stop targeting her—unless Mason gives up information on one of his clients.

Read on for a sneak preview of
MISTAKEN IDENTITY by **Shirlee McCoy,**
available March 2017 from Love Inspired Suspense!

Mason scanned the lake, then the trees behind them. "I don't like the feel of things. You have your phone?"

"Yes." Trinity fished it out of her pocket.

"Text your brother. Tell him to meet us down here—and to come armed."

She texted quickly, her fingers shaking with adrenaline and fear.

Chance texted back immediately and she tucked the phone away again. "He and Cyrus are on the way. He said to stay where we are."

"Where we are makes us sitting ducks." He stood, pulling her to her feet. "They want you, Trinity. I've got no doubt about that. They think they can use you as a pawn to get what they want from me."

"You're assuming someone is here. It's possible—"

The crack of gunfire split the air and she was on the ground, Mason covering her, her body pressed into the damp sand. She thought she heard an engine, but she couldn't hear much past the blood pulsing in her ears.

"Listen to me," Mason said, his mouth close to her ear. "They're coming down on mopeds. That's going to make it nearly impossible for them to get a clean shot. We've got to make it to the canoe and we've got to make it there quickly. You ready to run?"

She nodded because she couldn't get enough air in her lungs to speak. And then he was up, yanking her to her feet again, sprinting across the beach, the sound of pursuit growing louder behind them.

Mason pulled his knife from its ankle sheath, slashing the rope that held his boat to the spindly bushes that grew near the water's edge.

"Get in," he yelled, holding Trinity's arm as she hopped into the aluminum hull. He followed quickly, shoving away from the shore, moving them out into deeper water as quickly as he could. As soon as he was clear, he prepped the outboard motor, his eyes on the woods.

They weren't out of gunshot range yet. Not even close.

Don't miss
MISTAKEN IDENTITY by Shirlee McCoy,
available March 2017 wherever
Love Inspired® Suspense books and ebooks are sold.

www.LoveInspired.com

Sarah Varland lives near the mountains in Alaska, where she loves writing, hiking, kayaking and spending time with her family. She's happily married to her college sweetheart, John, and is the mom of two active and adorable boys, Joshua and Timothy, as well as another baby in heaven. Sarah has been writing almost since she could hold a pencil and especially loves writing romantic suspense, where she gets to combine her love for happily-ever-afters, inspired by her own, with her love for suspense, inspired by her dad, who has spent a career in law enforcement. You can find Sarah online through her blog, espressoinalatteworld.blogspot.com.

Books by Sarah Varland

Love Inspired Suspense

Treasure Point Secrets
Tundra Threat
Cold Case Witness
Silent Night Shadows
Perilous Homecoming

Visit the Author Profile page at Harlequin.com.

Brave. That was how Kelsey looked to Sawyer right now.

Brave.

Sawyer watched her draw in a breath, look behind her again and hurry toward him. When she finally reached his side she stopped.

"Are you okay?" he asked.

She shook her head. Then nodded. "I'm not sure. I'm alive, but..."

"But someone tried to kill you again."

Whoever this was meant business. Those notes weren't made to intimidate, weren't just bluffs. The killer had told her if she didn't leave town he'd kill her. Clearly he meant to follow through on his promise.

He glanced around. "You don't see anyone out there anymore, do you?"

"No, but that doesn't mean he's not hiding somewhere. I still don't know where he came from."

"Let's sit, then," Sawyer said.

Sawyer tried to keep his distance, or at least do the best he could when he was determined not to get farther than a couple of feet from her since she was in danger. But he wasn't touching her, wasn't even close.

Until he noticed her hand was shaking. Then he reached out and took it in his.